A place
to call home

JACKIE
FRENCH
KOLLER

A place
to call home

Aladdin Paperbacks

25 Years of Magical Reading

ALADDIN PAPERBACKS
EST. 1972

First Aladdin Paperbacks edition 1997
Copyright © 1995 by Jackie French Koller

Aladdin Paperbacks
An imprint of Simon & Schuster Children's Publishing Division
1230 Avenue of the Americas
New York, NY 10020

Also available in an Atheneum Books for Young Readers edition

Printed and bound in the United States of America
10 9 8 7 6 5 4 3 2 1

The Library of Congress has cataloged the hardcover edition as follows:
Koller, Jackie French.
A place to call home / by Jackie French Koller. — 1st ed.
p. cm.
Summary: Caring for her two younger siblings after their unreliable mother abandons them, fifteen-year-old Anna discovers the difficulties of trying to be a parent.
ISBN 0-689-80024-X
[1. Family problems—Fiction. 2. Mother and child—Fiction. 3. Afro-Americans—Fiction.] I. Title.
PZ7.K833Pl 1995
[Fic]—dc20 95-7559
IBSN 0-698-81395-3 (Aladdin pbk.)

*In loving memory of Mamére,
who had room enough in her heart
for all the world's children*

1

I am happy. The sun is shining and the air is sweet. I have pushed up the school bus window and fresh, spring warmth flows over me, ruffling my hair and brushing across my cheek like a silken scarf. The lawns we pass are slowly turning from brown to green, and if I look closely I can see a faint rosy tinge to the rolling, gray hills in the distance—billions of tiny buds, too new even to be green. It has been a long, hard winter and my heart can't help but be light on a day like this.

The bus slows, brakes squealing, and I am startled to see that we are approaching my driveway. I have been daydreaming again, and time has slipped away. I rise quickly and hoist my backpack onto my shoulder. It's heavy and I tilt my body to balance it. It is filled to bursting because I am always afraid that I will forget an assignment, or remember too late that I have a quiz coming up, so I bring home all my books, every night. Mama makes fun of me, calls me "Old Beggar Woman" because of the way the weight bows me over. I don't mind the weight, though. These books will one day set me free.

I start down the aisle, lurching a bit from the weight and the motion, and then, out of nowhere, a dog darts in front of the bus. The bus driver swears and slams hard on the brakes. I trip over someone's foot and the weight of my backpack shifts, throwing me off balance and pulling me after it into the nearest seat.

"Umph," I hear as I crash into someone's lap. My glasses fly off, and the strained clasp of my backpack gives way, spilling my books onto the floor. I bend to retrieve them and my hair clip catches on the seat in front of me, tugging loose, and tumbling my thick black hair down over my face. I am sweating now, burning with embarrassment.

"I'm sorry," I blurt out to whoever owns the lap I am struggling to get out of.

"That's all right," the lap's owner assures me.

It's a boy's voice, and there's laughter in it. I push my hair to one side and look into the freckled face of my neighbor, Nate Leon. My embarrassment deepens and Nate looks at me strangely, as if he is seeing something in me he's never seen before. The look makes me feel even warmer and I'm glad for my dark skin, glad he can't see how I'm blushing.

"I uh . . . think some of my books slid under the seat," I stammer.

"Here, let me help."

"No, that's okay."

Nate and I bend at the same time, clunking heads, and I wonder if this nightmare will ever end.

"Jeez, I'm sorry!" I cry, jumping out of Nate's lap and grabbing up the loose books. "That hurt, didn't it?"

"No," Nate says, but I can tell by the way he is rubbing his head that he's lying.

"Yes, it did," I insist, biting my lip.

"No, really, I'm fine. How about you?"

"Hey!" yells the bus driver, frowning into his rearview mirror. "Are you getting off or not?"

"Yes, I'm coming." I shove my books back into my bag and Nate hands me my glasses and my hair clip. I straighten up, feeling like Alice in Wonderland, growing taller and taller until I'm all out of proportion. Everyone is staring. "I'm sorry," I mumble.

"No problem." Nate chuckles. "Next time you want to sit with me though, just ask. I'll be happy to save you a seat."

Giggles break out all around me. I dash down the aisle and out the door.

The bus pulls away and I stand alone, surrounded by a cloud of dust and exhaust. My stomach churns at the smell, and I hold my breath until the wind blows the cloud away. Then I suck in a deep gulp of fresh air. It tastes sweet, like spring water from a tin cup, and I suck in another gulp to calm myself. My ears still smolder. What a klutz I am! I lower my heavy bag to the ground, twist my hair into a knot and replace my clip, then settle my glasses on my nose again. I think about myself as I was just a moment ago, sprawled across Nate Leon's lap. A small smile tugs at my lips. I've never been so close to a boy before. I've looked at them, though, and daydreamed about being close to one. I've looked at Nate a lot. He isn't like the other boys my age. There is something special about him, something quiet and deep.

Boys don't look back at me, though. I am scrawny and tall with wild black hair and glasses. I wear secondhand clothes from the Salvation Army and Mama's old shoes with tissue stuffed in the toes. The kids in school tease me and call me "Raggedy Anna" behind my back. I am black, too, but that's not the problem. There are only a handful of black kids in this town and most of them are rich, so the white kids go out of their way to be friendly with them. Ethnic diversity is "in" these days—as long as you're not poor. The kids in school think I'm odd because of the way I look, and because I keep to myself and always have my nose in a book. But that's okay. I think they're odd, too, with nothing better to do than talk about what's on TV, and who likes who.

Who likes who?

My scalp tingles at the memory of Nate's eyes smiling into mine. I hear the bus brake in the distance, and I steal a glance and see Nate jump from the steps. A little tremor of surprise flutters in my stomach. He is looking my way, too! I glance away, embarrassed, and hurry over to my mailbox, pretending to be busy with the mail. Curiosity gets the better of me, though, and my eyes flicker back in Nate's direction. He's still looking!

My hands turn clumsy, dropping the letters I pull from the box. I bend to pick them up and wonder why I'm so awkward. I don't look Nate's way again. I clutch the letters to my chest, retrieve my book bag from the dirt, and run up my driveway as fast as I can, anxious to be out of sight behind the trees. Why can't I be graceful, like the beautiful, young, black women I've seen on MTV, the elegant ones, who move like queens. Sometimes I take my glasses off, let my hair down, and pose in front of my bedroom mirror like an African queen. Without my glasses I can pretend that my blurry image is beautiful. Mama caught me posing that way once. She yanked me by one arm, twisted my hair back into its knot and pushed my glasses down hard on my nose.

"This is you, Anna O'Dell," she said, shoving me up close to the mirror. "Don't you go pretendin' to be somethin' else."

Mama doesn't want me to be beautiful, won't even let me try, but I don't know why. She was beautiful once. Before whiskey and cigarettes made her skin gray, and too much bleach turned her golden hair to lifeless yellow straw. When I was little I longed to be white-skinned, like Mama. I thought she might be happier with me then. But I know the truth now. My little brother and sister have white skin and she doesn't treat them any better than me. It isn't us Mama's not happy with. It's herself. But I don't know why. Mama is a puzzle too hard for me to solve.

I don't care what she thinks, though. I want to be beautiful anyway. I want to be rid of these Coke-bottle glasses, and have pretty clothes to wear, and have boys look at me like . . . like . . . Was it my imagination, or was Nate Leon looking at me that way on the bus just now, as if he glimpsed, if only for a moment, the beauty in me . . . ?

I'm out of breath when I finally reach the cover of the trees and I have to laugh at myself. Beauty indeed! Squiggles of hair still cling to my face and my glasses are sliding off the end of my clammy nose. I push them back into place and wipe sweat from my brow with my jacket sleeve. I can relax now. My dirt driveway is long and winding. Once past the curtain of trees it is private and I can forget about the world outside and live in my world, a world of stories and dreams. I dream now about Nate, letting myself believe that he was looking at me in that special way, the way a boy looks when he is interested in a girl. . . .

I am fifteen, and I have never kissed a boy. I have thought about it often, though, and I have practiced, on the bathroom mirror and on my teddy bear, Clark. But those kinds of kisses only leave me feeling empty. A real kiss would feel soft and silky, I think, and fill up the hollow places inside me with warmth. I close my eyes and dream of kissing Nate, of looking deep into those mysterious, green eyes. . . .

"Ooof!" My toe thuds into something hard and pain jolts through my foot. I stagger forward and fall to my knees in the dirt, the mail fluttering down around me. Tears sting my eyes and I smack the dirt hard with my open hand.

A gloom settles over me. What is the sense of dreaming anyway? Mama will never let me have a boyfriend, or even a friend for that matter. She doesn't like strangers, doesn't want anyone coming around, "poking into our business." I sigh and pick up the bills that lay scattered about.

Warning! Warning! Final notice! I stuff the bills into my backpack. I don't want to think about them now. I want my happiness back. I force myself to think of happy things, the A+ I got on my Spanish test today, and the fact that there are only two more tests and two more days of school to go before April vacation. I sniff the air again and turn my face up to the sun. Its warmth soothes me.

I get to my feet again and trudge the rest of the way up the driveway. The clearing comes into view, and in its center, the little house that I share with my mother, little sister, and baby brother.

I've grown fond of this house in the two years we have lived here. It's nothing to look at. The old asbestos shingles are a mustard yellow that must have been ugly, even when new, and the roof has been patched so many times, it looks like a faded crazy quilt. The porch slumps and the shutters sag, and tattered shades hang low in the windows, like drooping eyelids. The yard has gone wild, ringed in by a rotting picket fence that rambles drunkenly along the edges, its once white coat of paint nothing but a milky gray memory. Old barrels, broken toys, and rusted car parts spill out of the yard, across the driveway, and into the woods beyond. The neighbors would object if they could see it from the street, but they can't, and so it remains, a reminder that Westbridge and the other hill towns in this northwestern corner of Connecticut weren't always as wealthy as they are today.

I would love to fix this house up, paint it, and patch it, and clean out the yard. . . . But we don't have the money, and Mama doesn't have the will, so it just keeps getting shabbier. That's okay, though. It's still a home and I'm glad to have one. There have been times when we O'Dells haven't been so lucky.

I smile to see that Mama's old yellow station wagon isn't in the driveway, happy at the thought of having the house to myself for a while. Privacy is a rare treat in this three-room bungalow. I hop up onto the porch, pull open the creaky skeleton of what used to be a screened door, and push my key into the rusty lock.

A small sound squeezes out through the wooden door and I turn instinctively to catch it in my ear. I catch only the trailing end of it, but it's enough to trigger an alarm inside my head. It's my baby brother, Casey, inside, crying.

And Mama's car is gone.

My happiness evaporates and my heart begins to thump. Casey's cry comes again, and anger tightens my chest. "Not again, Mama," I hiss through clenched teeth as I jiggle my key in the unyielding lock. My anger deepens, fueled by frustration. "Open, dammit!" I shout.

At last the lock gives, and I burst through the door, dropping my book bag to the floor.

"Mama?" I shout. "Mama, are you here?"

Casey's cries are the only answer. I race into the bedroom and find him writhing in his crib. His hands and feet flail in the air. His face is beet red, and he is choking on his tears.

I grab him up and hug him close.

"Shh, shhush. It's okay, baby," I say softly.

He clings to me like a frightened kitten, his hands clutching at my jacket, his head burrowing into my chest. He quiets for a moment and pulls back, looking at me with desperate eyes.

I sigh heavily. "She's gone again, isn't she?" I whisper.

Though I know he doesn't understand, Casey's face crinkles up and his tears begin anew.

"Okay, okay," I whisper, rubbing his back as I carry him out to the kitchen. "Anna's here. Hush now." I pull open the refrigerator door. No formula. Why am I not surprised? Nothing to drink but an open, half-empty bottle of 7up.

I search the cupboards, but there is no formula there either.

"Well," I say as I pull the 7up from the refrigerator, "at least it's flat. It won't give you gas this time."

I carry the bottle over and sit it down on the counter, then fish with my free hand under the stack of dirty dishes in the sink, wrinkling my nose at the smell of old food. I find a baby bottle, but when I finally manage to unscrew the nipple, a sour, cheesy smell assaults my nose.

"I'm sorry, Casey," I say, "but I'm going to have to put you down for a minute." I walk over and sit him in his playpen. He gives me a startled look, as if he has been betrayed, then his arms flail out and he begins to kick and squall, falling backward into his blankets. His desperation unnerves me, and I hurry back to the sink, sweat breaking out on my upper lip as I rush to scrub out and fill the bottle. I dash back, scoop Casey up again, and shove the bottle into his mouth. The screaming ceases instantly, and with a sigh of relief I carry him into the living room and sink down on the sofa.

He sucks greedily, gulping and gulping, laboring to breathe through his runny nose. He pauses now and then, just long enough to suck in a big breath of air before hungrily attacking the nipple again. A pile of unfolded laundry sits on the other end of the sofa, and I lean over and pull out a washcloth. I wipe Casey's nose, then dab at a little tear that has pooled in the small depression between his eye and the bridge of his nose. He is shuddering less now, and the red flush is fading from his skin, all except for a welt across his forehead. I wince, remembering how Mama lost her temper this morning and hit him.

"Poor little Casey," I whisper, caressing his tiny white fingers. "It's been a rough seven months, hasn't it?"

He stares up at me, his big, blue eyes probing mine, questioning.

I wish I had answers for him, but I'm frightened, too. Mama hasn't been this bad since Mandy was a baby. I don't know what lies ahead. I know one thing, though. I will not tell this time, will not watch them come and tear this baby from Mama's arms, will not stand there and have her turn to me with tears running down her cheeks and cry, "Who told, Anna? Who told? No one knew but you!"

I brush Casey's soft cheek with my finger. "You can trust me, Casey," I tell him. "I'll never hurt you and I'll never leave you. Go to sleep now. Anna is here."

2

Casey has fallen so soundly asleep that I'm
sure he must have been crying for hours. He is
as limp as a rag doll. Once he is changed and
tucked in I have time to think. I search the
house for a sign of what has happened to Mama,
a note perhaps, or some indication of where she
went, but there is nothing. No clothes are missing from her closet, and the old brown suitcase
is still shoved under the bed, covered in dust.
She hasn't gone far then, I tell myself. She'll be
back soon.

On the kitchen table I find an empty whiskey
bottle. Maybe that's it. Mama ran out of booze
and went to get more? No. In that case she
would have taken Casey, or waited until I got
home. She's just run out again, out to wherever
it is she runs when things get to be too much for
her. A man probably. There have been many
men. When I was small we lived with them
sometimes, until that night. She was working
and I had a bad dream and crawled into bed

beside the man. Mama went crazy when she came home, screamed and smashed things and chased the man out of the house. I've always felt bad for that man. I don't think he even knew I was there.

There have been men since, obviously. Mandy and Casey are proof of that. But Mama doesn't bring them home anymore. Won't even speak of them, answers my questions only with a cold, gray stare.

How long will she be gone this time? I wonder. A few hours, a night, a day or two? She has been disappearing almost as long as I can remember. My heart still aches, remembering the first time. . . .

They placed me in a big family with lots of other children, and I didn't see Mama for weeks. The house was full of laughter and noise, but I cried every night. The mother held me in her lap and rocked me and called me Little Angel, but I only wanted my own mama. When I finally got her back I held onto her so tight that my fingers made little blue bruises on her skin.

I was five years old.

I'm not frightened like that anymore. I've learned to take care of myself, and when the little ones came, I learned to take care of them, too. There are tricks, ways of hiding the truth, and I know them all. I'm angry, though. More than angry. Furious. Furious that Mama does this to us, again and again. Sooner or later the people in this town will begin to wonder, just like in all the other towns we've lived in. They'll start asking questions, and then, before the questions get too hard to answer, we'll be moving on.

My stomach winds up into a knot at the thought. Another new school, another new town . . . I don't want to leave this little house. I stare out of the kitchen window at the empty driveway.

"Come home, Mama," I whisper. "Please, just come home."

But Mama doesn't come, and I know I can't afford to wait. I drag a kitchen chair over to the counter and climb up and pull the emergency coffee can off the top shelf. I lift the plastic lid and look inside. Good. At least she didn't take all the money this time. I jump down and dump the can out on the counter. A little pile of coins clink out and I grab a quarter that rolls toward the sink. The bills and food stamps stick inside the can and I pull them out and flatten them. There are seventeen dollars' worth, and the change comes to two dollars and sixty-three cents. Just under twenty dollars in total. We can last for a while on that.

I check the cupboards again, this time looking for food. There isn't much left, and Casey will need formula when he wakes up. I'll have to walk to the convenience store on the corner when Mandy gets home. I look at the pile of dishes in the sink. At least I'll have a chance to clean the place up a little without Mama scowling behind my back, telling me one mother in a house is enough.

Yes, Mama. It would be, if we had one we could count on.

My eyes fall upon my book bag, still lying on the floor where I dropped it, and my heart sinks. What will I do about school if Mama doesn't come back? I have a history test tomorrow, and I have to get an A. It's part of my plan. I'm almost through with my sophomore year, and I haven't gotten a grade lower than an A yet. I'm going to get A's all the way through high school, and win a full scholarship to college. I want to be a writer, but I know I'll have to do something else, too, something that makes money. Maybe I'll be a teacher, or a lawyer, at least until my books become famous. I may even come back here to Westbridge one day and live in a house you can see from the street. I'll take care of Mandy and Casey, and yes, Mama, too. Mama will be different then. She won't have any worries, so she won't have to drink anymore, and she won't get angry and mean and run away. Maybe . . . maybe she'll even remember how to smile. . . .

I will study later, when the little ones are in bed, study all night if I have to, until I know the material backward and forward. And if Mama doesn't come home, I'll worry about what to do in the morning. There is enough to worry about now. Besides, Mama might come back tonight. You just never know.

I open the kitchen window, and the spring breeze drifts in. The thin curtains lift up their ragged ends and dance, and I smile in spite of myself. That is what I love about the world. Even in the hardest of times, there are moments of joy. I wish I could make Mama see them.

I turn the radio on softly, fill the sink with lemon-scented suds and dive in up to my elbows. I hum along with the radio, letting the music fill my head and the breeze caress my face. Now I'm dancing, dancing under the stars, and it's Nate's hand caressing my cheek, touching me softly as we dance. . . .

A low rumble penetrates my dreams and my eyes dart to the driveway. It isn't Mama's car, though. It's the school bus out on the main road, and soon Mandy comes around the bend, swinging her lunch box and singing at the top of her lungs.

I smile. It is a day for singing, and I don't want it to be ruined for her. I will try, like I always try, to keep her the way she is at this moment. Oblivious. Sheltered from the truth, buffered from the pain. I will keep her that way as long as I can.

She pushes her way exuberantly through the

kitchen door and throws her little arms around my middle.

"Hi, Anna," she says, squeezing me tight. "Wanna see my pitchur?"

"Sure," I tell her, wiping down my soapy arms and bending over to kiss the top of her little blond head.

She shakes off her jacket, then plops down in the middle of the floor and unsnaps her lunch box.

I wince. "Mandy, don't sit on the floor," I say, "it's filthy."

"Mommy lets me," she says.

Her answer irritates me more than it should. "I know," I snap, "but Mommy's not here right now and I'm in charge."

A shadow darkens Mandy's bright expression. "Where's Mommy?" she asks.

"She . . . went out."

"Out where?"

"I don't know. Nowhere important. She'll be back soon."

Mandy looks unconvinced and I'm annoyed with myself for planting this worry in her head.

"So, where's this work of art?" I quip, hoping to draw her attention away from the subject of Mama. It works and Mandy begins digging again through the papers in her lunch box.

"Here it is!" she says, pulling out a piece of rumpled newsprint. She unfolds it and holds up something that looks like a big pepperoni pizza with thick drips of dried poster paint running down from it.

"Why, what a beautiful . . . flower," I say. Flower is usually a pretty safe bet. Mandy is fond of flowers and loves to paint them in all sizes, shapes, and colors. But not today.

"It's not a flower," she says in a wounded voice. "It's Casey!"

"Oh, Casey!" I cry. "Of course. Now I see." I take the picture from Mandy and hold it up. "It looks just like him," I say. "I don't know how I could have made such a mistake."

Mandy shakes her head in bewilderment. "You must be just dumb," she says.

I smile. "Guess so."

Mandy reaches up and grabs the painting. "I'm gonna show Casey hisself," she says, dashing back toward the bedroom.

I dart after her. "No, Mandy, wait!" I call, but she ignores me. I catch hold of her shirt just outside of the bedroom door, yank her to a halt, and scoop her up.

"Hey!" she screams. "I said I wanna . . ."

I clap a hand over her mouth and carry her, kicking and squirming, back out to the kitchen. Suddenly I feel a sharp twinge of pain in the palm of my hand.

"Ouch!" I cry, dropping her to the floor. "You bit me, you little sh . . ." I catch myself before the word comes out and stare down into Mandy's sullen face. ". . . brat!" I say instead.

"You were gonna call me a bad word," Mandy accuses.

"I was not."

"Were too."

"Was not."

"Were too!"

I roll my eyes. I am arguing with a five-year-old. "All right," I admit. "I was going to call you a bad word. I'm sorry."

"I thought you didn't like bad words," says Mandy.

"I don't."

"Then why did you almost call me one?"

"Because you bit me, you little pain!"

Mandy's eyes widen. "Milly Thompson bit me yesterday," she says. "Tomorrow I'm gonna call her a . . ."

"Mandy!" I interrupt. "You are not going to call her any such thing. You're not to use those words. Do you hear me?"

"Why not?"

Because swearing is crude, I want to tell her, and because people expect it from people like us, and I will not give them the satisfaction of being what they expect. I will tell her this some day, but not yet. She doesn't know yet that we are different. "Because it's not nice to say bad words," I tell her. "That's why I stopped myself and didn't say what I was going to say."

Mandy considers this a moment, then sticks out her bottom lip.

"Mommy says bad words all the time," she says.

I frown. *Exactly,* I think to myself. But I don't tell Mandy this either. "I know," I say tiredly, "but that doesn't mean we should."

"Why not?"

"You know why . . . because . . . Mommy does a lot of things that aren't very good."

Mandy's expression grows grave. "Like hitting?" she says.

I reach out and touch her hair. "Yes," I say, "like that."

Mandy looks up into my eyes. "Is Mommy a bad person?" she asks.

I look away so Mandy won't see the answer that smolders within me. Yes, I want to say. She's a mean, terrible, selfish person, and I hate her! But as soon as I say "I hate her!" inside my head, I feel ashamed. Guilty over my anger. I think about all of Mama's tearful promises, the agony in her face whenever she comes home, saying, "Never, Anna. Never again. You'll see."

Yes, Mama. I see. I see better than you.

I feel tears starting in the corners of my eyes, but I blink them away. Mandy still waits. I turn to smooth a strand of hair out of her face and force a smile from somewhere deep inside myself.

"Mama doesn't mean to be bad," I tell her gently. "She just can't help herself sometimes. That's why we have to be very patient with her."

Mandy nods solemnly. Her eyes reflect a wisdom far beyond her years, and in that reflection I see the truth of my own words. I let the last of my anger go, relieved to be free of the weight of it.

"Can I show Casey his pitchur now?" Mandy asks.

"Pic-ture," I correct her, shaking my head.

"Why not?" Mandy stamps her foot.

"Shush." I put a finger to my lips. "Casey is very tired," I explain, "and I want him to get some rest."

"But I wanna play with him now," Mandy insists. She draws the word "now" out into a long, annoying whine.

"No!" I tell her firmly, but she ignores me and goes on whining. She grabs my hand in both of hers and shakes it up and down.

"Plea-eese," she begs.

My patience snaps and I pull my hand loose. "Mandy, just stop!" I tell her. "Casey is not one of your dolls. If you wake him up now he'll whine and cry and be a pain, but if you let him sleep he'll wake up happy. Then he'll smile and giggle for you later."

Mandy pouts for a while, then looks up at me sullenly. "Can we play peekaboo with him when he wakes up?" she asks.

"Sure," I tell her. "He'll like that. But right now I have a special job for you."

Mandy's eyes brighten. "What is it?"

"I need you to baby-sit for a few minutes while I run to the corner store."

Mandy frowns in disappointment. She's had to do this job before. It's not her idea of special.

"I'll pay you," I say.

Her eyes brighten once more. "You will?"

"Yes," I tell her, "I'll pay you one Sugar Daddy lollipop!"

"Aw-right!" she shouts.

"Shush!" I remind her.

Mandy hunches up her shoulders and presses her own finger to her lips. Then she makes a twisting motion like she is locking her lips and throwing away the key.

"Okay, good," I tell her. "Now, I won't be long. Remember the rules. If anybody comes to the door, hide and pretend you're not home, and if anybody calls on the phone, tell them your mommy's in the shower. Got it?"

Mandy nods, her lips pursed tight together.

"And don't wake Casey up."

Mandy gives me the "okay" sign.

I smile and chuck her under the chin. "That's my little monkey," I whisper.

3

I walk up and down the aisles of Mel's Convenience Store grumbling under my breath. I hate shopping here. Everything is so expensive! I pick up a can of premixed formula, frown at the price, and put it back again. Then I pick up a can of powdered mix. It's a better buy because it makes more, but because it's a larger size it costs more. I spend a long time debating the choice.

"Can I help you?"

Mel leans over his register, watching me like he's afraid I'm trying to steal something.

"Yeah. You can stop robbing people," I say.

Mel looks startled. "Hey," he says, his thick, gray brows arching up in indignation, "whaddaya mean?"

I pick a box of rice out of the basket that hangs from my arm and shake it at him. "I paid a dollar," I tell him, "a whole dollar less for this same size at Big Mart last month. Your prices are outrageous!"

Mel sucks in a deep breath and lets it out slowly, regaining his composure in the process. "Hey," he says. "Nobody's twisting your arm. If you'd rather go to Big Mart, go to Big Mart. It's no skin off my nose."

"I can't get to Big Mart right now," I tell him.

He smiles. "Well, that's the point, isn't it?" he says. "That's why it's called Mel's Convenience Store."

I shake my head, load the premixed formula and a package of diapers into my basket, then huff over to the register. Mel starts taking things out and ringing them up.

"Eighty-nine cents!" I shriek when he rings up the macaroni and cheese. "They're three for a dollar at Big Mart!"

Mel pauses with the macaroni box in hand and looks at me strangely. "You give me the creeps, you know that, kid," he says, "comin' in here, complainin' all the time. You sound like some old, pain-in-the-arse lady, and Lord knows I got enough of them to put up with."

"Well," I tell him, "maybe if you lowered your prices . . ."

Mel thumps the macaroni box back down on the counter. "Look," he says, "I gotta make a livin', too, you know? In case you didn't notice, that ain't no Cadillac I got parked outside."

We stare at each other in silence for a moment, then Mel shakes his head and goes back to ringing up the order. What he says is true, I suppose. His car is old, and the apartment he and his wife live in up over the store is probably not luxurious, but it's hard for me to be sympathetic. All I care about right now is my family and all I know is that Mel's prices are making my life harder.

"Twelve dollars and twenty-seven cents," he says when he is through. I scowl at the total but say nothing more as Mel loads the groceries into a sack. I count out the precious stamps and bills.

"Thank you," Mel says with exaggerated sweetness. "Have a nice day."

I pick up the sack and start to walk out the door when I spy the candy counter and remember Mandy's Sugar Daddy. I take one from the rack and hold it up.

"How much for this?" I ask.

"Sixty cents," says Mel.

"Sixty cents!"

Mel rolls his eyes up toward the ceiling. I let out a great sigh, plunk the groceries and the lollipop down on the counter and start to pull the few remaining bills back out of my pocket. Suddenly Mel reaches across the counter, grabs the lollipop, and tosses it into the sack.

"Forget it," he says.

"Forget what?"

"The money for the lollipop. Just take it."

"I will not . . ."

"Oh, yes you will." Mel comes out from behind the counter, grabs my bag, stuffs it into my arms and escorts me to the door.

"Well . . . all right," I agree reluctantly. "Thanks . . . for the Sugar Daddy, I mean."

"Yeah, yeah. Don't mention it. Just do me a favor."

"What?" I ask, expecting him to say, "Next time go to Big Mart."

"Try and remember how to be a kid," says Mel.

I scuff along in the gutter, a winter's worth of soft, salty sand shifting beneath the soles of my shoes.

Try and remember how to be a kid.

I step on the grate of a culvert and stop suddenly, looking down. And I do remember. Feet so small my insides tickle with fear at the thought of slipping down between the bars of the grate. Holding Mama's hand, just to be safe. Crouching over. Peering into the darkness. Lovely, deep, mysterious darkness. Finding a pebble. Letting it fall. Listening to the splash, somewhere way down below. A cool, echo-y sound. Feeling happy, just because of the sound. Finding another pebble, letting it fall . . .

I push up a ridge of sand with the top of my shoe, guide it to the edge of the grate, and over.

Th . . . wisshh, goes the sand, hitting the water far below. I laugh and push up another ridge, then suddenly I straighten up, my face flushing at the thought of Mandy and Casey, waiting, home alone.

"Stupid," I chide myself, giving the sand an angry kick. But I pause just long enough to hear the *th . . . wisshh* once more before I run home.

4

Everything looks calm and ordinary as I hurry up the driveway, but there is still no sign of Mama's station wagon. I hop up onto the porch and knock softly on the kitchen door so as not to wake Casey. No one answers, but I hear the Barney theme song blaring from the TV. I cup a hand over my eyes to block out the light and peer in through the window just in time to see Mandy dash by the open doorway to the living room, pulling something behind her. She is giggling hysterically. I shake my head in good-natured frustration. So much for Mandy's promise to keep quiet. If Casey isn't awake already, he'll be up any second.

I rap louder on the door, but Mandy still doesn't hear me. She runs past the doorway again, and this time I get a look at her "pull-toy."

"Oh no!" I shriek. "Mandy, stop!" I put the grocery bag on the ground and fish out my key. "I'm going to kill her," I mumble under my breath as I fiddle with the lock. "One of these days I'm really going to kill her!"

The lock gives way and I run straight through the kitchen and into the living room.

"Amanda Abigail O'Dell!" I shriek. "Let that baby go!"

Mandy pauses only a second in her race around the living room. "He likes it," she yells. "See!"

She is off again, pulling Casey behind her on his back by the drawstring at the bottom of his sleeping gown. And indeed, he *does* seem to be liking it. He giggles, arms waving excitedly as his head bumps over the ridges in our old, braided rug. Mandy rounds the corner and I suck in my breath as Casey's head narrowly misses the leg of the coffee table.

"Mandy, stop it!" I shout. "I don't care if he does like it. Stop it this minute!"

Mandy's steps slow and she turns to cast a sullen glance at me as the baby bumps to a halt behind her.

"Why?" she asks.

I run over and pick Casey up, checking his head for new bruises. "Why?" I echo, looking at Mandy in horror. "Why? Because he's a baby, not a toy! Do you want to break his head open?"

Mandy sticks out her bottom lip. "I didn't break him," she pouts.

"No," I admit, "thank God, but you might have if I hadn't come home just now. That was very naughty, Mandy. And to think I trusted you with a grown-up job."

Resentful tears well in Mandy's eyes. "I was just trying to make him happy," she argues. "He was crying and crying . . ."

Anger rises inside me, but not at Mandy, at Mama. I know all too well how desperate Casey gets when he is hungry. It's unfair to give Mandy such responsibility, and Mandy knows it's unfair, but she thinks I'm the one to blame. She stares at me now, accusingly.

"I'm sorry," I tell her. "You're right. It's not your fault. Casey's not hurt, so we'll just forget about it, okay?"

Mandy continues to sulk.

"Do I still get paid?" she asks.

I smile. "Yes," I say, "if you promise never to use Casey as a pull-toy again."

Mandy smiles at last. "I promise," she says, clapping her hands.

"Okay," I tell her. "Go bring in the grocery bag from the front porch and then you can have your Sugar Daddy."

Mandy dashes away and Casey starts to fuss in my arms. I carry him out to the kitchen, shove aside the rack of clean dishes I left on the counter and lay him down. Mandy struggles in and deposits the grocery bag on a kitchen chair.

"Good girl," I tell her. "Get out your lollipop, then run and get me a clean diaper, please."

I untie Casey's sleeper and undo his wet diaper. As I reach for the washcloth a little stream of yellow pee arches up into the air, right past my nose, and then sprinkles down again—all over my rack of clean dishes!

"Oh, Casey!" I shriek.

My cry startles him. His arms flail out, his eyes go wide, and his lip quivers pathetically, tugging at my heartstrings, before he bursts into frightened tears.

"What's the matter with Casey?" cries Mandy, running back out into the kitchen with the diaper in her hand.

"I scared him," I confess, gathering Casey up and trying my best to calm him again.

Mandy puts one hand on her hip and waves her lollipop at me. "That's very naughty, Anna," she scolds, "and to think Mommy trusted you with a grown-up job."

I give her a wry smile. "Very funny," I say. "Just hand me the diaper, will you?"

"It's the last one," says Mandy.

"I know." I frown as I take the diaper from her. "I just bought another package. Babies are so expensive. Mommy better come home before we run out . . ."

"What?" asks Mandy.

A nervous flush races up my neck and the roots of my hair tingle. I've just blown it.

"What did you say?" Mandy asks again, her

voice suddenly small and timid. "Isn't Mommy coming home?"

I glance at her quickly. "Coming home?" I say. "Of course she's coming home. It's just that she may be . . . very late. She has to go to . . . a meeting, I think. A PTA meeting."

"A what?" Mandy asks.

"A parent-teacher meeting . . . at school tonight. I think she was planning to . . . have dinner out and then go to the meeting, and . . . she was going to pick up some more diapers, too. That's what I was saying—I hope she gets home before we run out of diapers again." I realize I'm babbling. I try changing the subject. "There now," I say, "Casey's all changed. Would you do me a big favor and make funny faces for him while I fix his bottle?"

Mandy is staring at me. *PTA meeting?* her eyes plainly say. *Give me a break, Anna.* She doesn't ask any more questions, though, and when I lower Casey into his playpen, she dutifully goes over and starts sticking out her candy-coated tongue and making her famous monkey sounds.

"That's it," I say, giving her a wink as Casey starts to grin.

I hurry back over to the sink and begin preparing Casey's bottle.

"Eep, eep, eep," sings Mandy, hopping around the playpen, scratching under her arms like a chimpanzee. Casey giggles, a sweet, baby giggle. "Eep, eep," Mandy continues. "Eep, eep . . . Eeyooo peeyooo gross!"

I turn from the sink.

"Now what?" I ask.

"Casey just did a big yellow poop," Mandy yells, "and it's sqwooshing out all over!"

I turn back to the sink, slump over, rest both elbows on the counter and bury my face in my hands.

No wonder Mama runs away.

The laundry is done, the little ones fed and bathed, the dishes washed and put away. The whole house has been vacuumed, Casey is tucked in, and I am just finishing mopping up the kitchen floor. I'm tired, but it makes me feel good when things are neat and tidy like this. Besides, the work has kept me from watching the clock and running to the window every time I hear a car engine in the distance.

Mandy patters out into the kitchen in her nightgown.

"There," I say, sweeping my arm in an arc across the room. "Doesn't everything look nice?"

Mandy surveys my handiwork unenthusiastically.

"What's wrong?" I ask.

"Mommy will be mad," she says.

"Oh, baloney," I tell her. "What's to be mad

about? Everything looks great."

Mandy twists her arms behind her back and digs at a hole in the linoleum with her bare big toe. "Mommy always gets mad when you clean," she said. "Mommy says she can do it."

I snort in disdain.

"Mommy says you're too bossy," Mandy continues.

"Well, somebody has to be in charge," I tell her. "Mommy sure isn't most of the time." I open the front door and put the wet mop out on the porch. When I turn back again, Mandy is in the same spot, still digging at the hole with her toe. She glances up at me through a damp fringe of bangs.

"I don't like it when Mommy yells at you," she says.

I go over, slip my hands under her spindly arms and hoist her up onto my hip.

"She's not going to yell at me, worrywart," I tell her gently. "Come on now, off to bed. I'll read you a story."

I carry Mandy into the bedroom and plunk her down on the double bed we share. Casey's breathing comes soft and regular from his crib in the corner.

"Pick out a story," I whisper as I switch on the small lamp beside the bed and turn down the covers.

Mandy scrambles down to the foot of the bed

and selects a little blue book from the pile on the old hope chest. I smile sadly when I see it.

"*The Runaway Bunny?*" I ask.

Mandy nods and curls into the crook of my arm. She smells like Ivory soap and baby powder, and her hair falls in damp ringlets over my arm. I give her a little squeeze, then open the book and begin the story of the little bunny who wants to run away, and the mother rabbit who promises that she will take him back, time after time after time.

"Once there was a little bunny who wanted to run away," I read, but it's not my voice I hear in my head. It is Mama's soft, southern drawl. And it's not Mandy's tiny body I see in my mind, and close beneath the covers, but my own. I'm a little girl again, and Mama is my world. And it is storytime. The magic time. The time when I have Mama close and safe and nothing exists but our two hearts, beating side by side.

I turn the pages slowly as we near the end of the story. I don't want it to be over. "Shucks," I hear Mama's voice say, "Ah might just as well stay where Ah am and be yore little bunny." I stare at the picture of the mother bunny, paws out, waiting to hug her child.

Yes, Mama, please stay.

"Anna?"

I jump, startled by the voice. I stare down into a pair of puzzled eyes and I'm confused for a

moment. Who is this little stranger, this inter-
loper . . . taking Mama's place?

"Anna?" Mandy says again. "What's wrong?"

I shake my head and the mist clears. Mandy's
worried face comes sharply into focus.

"What's wrong?" she repeats.

"Wrong? Nothing's wrong." I hear my own
voice now. It sounds strangely loud in my ears.

"But, you didn't finish," says Mandy.

"Oh . . . oh, yes." I clear my throat and begin
to read again. This time the voice I hear is my
own.

"I might just as well stay where I am and be
your little bunny," I read. "And so he did. 'Have
a carrot,' said the mother bunny."

Mandy reaches over and turns the final page
and we both gaze at the picture of the little
bunny and his mother, safe and snug together,
down below the garden in their cozy den.

"The mother bunny is *very* patient, isn't she,"
Mandy says softly.

"Yes." I sigh and nod. "Very patient."

Mandy looks up at me. "Just like we have to
be with Mommy, huh?"

A lump forms in my throat and my eyes grow
moist. "Yes," I whisper hoarsely, "just like we
have to be with Mommy."

5

I feel pain. At first I think I'm dreaming it, but the pain keeps intruding on my dreams until I must acknowledge it. My neck is twisted at an odd angle and my eyeglass frames are cutting into my cheek. I turn my head and a shaft of light stabs at my eyes. I'm confused. Where am I? What is this light? I open my eyes a crack, blocking the light with my hand. I find myself curled up in the living room chair, the light streaming in through a hole in the shade. I snatch a throw pillow from behind my back and pull it over my face, but the pillow smells of stale smoke and mildew and it makes me choke. When I pull it away again, a thousand sparkling dust motes swim before my eyes. In exasperation I throw my pillow at the hole in the shade and sit up. The pillow bounces off the window and lands on the TV, knocking a pile of magazines onto the rug.

I rub my aching neck and my eyes focus on my history book, lying open on the floor. I stare at it stupidly for a moment and then I remember.

My head jerks up and I stare at the couch. It's still folded up, unslept in. I stand up, ignore my cramped and aching body, and tiptoe back to the bedroom. Perhaps Mama came home, saw me in the chair, and went in to sleep with Mandy. I push the door open a crack and peek in, praying that I will see two bumps in the bed.

There is but one small one.

I gently close the door again and lean against the frame, my heart sinking. For a moment all the old fears come back. What if something has happened? What if Mama is hurt? What if she doesn't come back? What if . . .

I draw in a deep breath and push the fears away. I cannot think these things. She *will* come back. She always has. Back with her lies and excuses. Back with her tears and promises . . .

Anger replaces fear and I feel in control again.

Dammit, Mama! How could you? How could you do this to me now? You couldn't wait two more lousy days?!

I storm out to the kitchen and check the clock on the wall. Six A.M. Well, I have some time to think, at least, before the babies wake up and the school busses arrive. I take a quick shower, get dressed, and then pull a piece of paper from my notebook.

"Anna cannot attend school today," I write, "because I have a sick migraine and I need her to watch her brother. Please send her homework home." I sign my mother's name with perfect accuracy. Forgery is one of the tricks I've learned. Then I fold the note angrily. I have never missed a day of school on my own. Never. I would have perfect attendance as well as perfect grades if not for Mama.

I close my eyes and bitter tears sting the lids. Why do I have to care so much? Why can't I just be aimless and indifferent, like she is. Then it wouldn't be so bad. I can't, though. I'm so unlike her that it's hard to believe we're mother and daughter. Maybe I take after my father, whoever he is, wherever he may be. . . . This need to achieve, this sense of right and wrong must come from somewhere. Certainly not from Mama.

I whisper to myself the words of a small poem I wrote years ago, a poem I call "Daddy."

Daddy, do you know you have a daughter?
Do you know she's just like you?
Would you love her if you knew?

The bedroom door opens in the hall and I turn. Mandy makes her way to the kitchen, rubbing sleep from her eyes. She gazes up at me, then looks quickly around the kitchen, into the living room, and back.

"Mommy?" she asks. I shake my head slowly from side to side.

Mandy's shoulders sag. She stares at the floor and brings her thumb to her mouth.

"She'll be home soon, Monk," I tell her. "Come give me a morning hug."

Mandy comes over and I hoist her up. She wraps her arms around my neck and squeezes me, then pulls back and looks into my face. "We'll be okay," she says, searching my eyes for confirmation.

"Of course we will," I tell her. "We can take care of ourselves."

"Yeah." Mandy nods, more confident now. "And we can take care of Casey, too, 'cause we're big."

"That's right," I say, lowering her to the floor again. "And the first thing big girls do in the morning is wash up and get dressed for school."

Mandy's confidence crumbles. "I don't wanna go to school," she says.

"Of course you do."

"No, I don't," Mandy repeats.

"Why not?" I ask. "You love school."

"I know," she says, "but . . . I need to stay here. I need to help you."

She is clinging to my arm now, her fingers making little pale dents in my skin. I understand her feelings all too well.

"Mandy," I say gently, "I'll be here when you get home. I promise."

Mandy shakes her head. "No," she says, her

voice coming out in a rush, "the social people might come. They'll find out Mommy's gone and they'll take you. . . ."

Mandy starts to cry and I pull her close and hug her. "Who told you about the social people?" I ask quietly.

"I heard Mommy yesterday . . . when she told you . . . not to tell . . . about Casey . . . about the hitting."

Mandy chokes out the words between sobs and my anger rises. Mandy isn't oblivious—she knows. I have tried to protect her, but she knows. There is no safety, not for the O'Dells.

I sigh deeply. The time for truth has come. I had hoped it could be put off a few more years, but the half-truths that Mandy knows now are dangerous.

"They are called social service people," I tell her, "and they aren't bad or mean or anything. They try to help people. It's just that, if they knew about Mommy, they would take us away from her and try to find homes for us. And there aren't many homes with space for three kids."

Mandy's eyes are riveted on mine. "So what would they do?" she asks.

"They would probably put us in different homes," I say.

Mandy's fingers claw into my skin.

"That's why they must never know," I go on. "You've got to go to school, just like everything is fine, and you have to laugh and play like always, so no one will guess that Mommy's not home."

"But what about you?" Mandy asks. "What if you don't go to school?"

"It'll be okay," I tell her. "They know Mommy gets sick a lot, and they know I have to watch Casey when she does." A bitter edge creeps into my voice. "They know I'd never skip school on my own."

"But what if Mommy doesn't come back soon?" asks Mandy. "What then?"

I look down into her worried face. "Next week is vacation anyway," I remind her, "and Mommy will surely be back before school starts again."

Mandy lowers her eyes. "I wish we had a daddy," she says softly.

My heart squeezes. "A daddy?" I repeat.

Mandy looks up at me and nods. "Like the other kids in school," she says. "If we had a daddy, he would take care of us when Mommy goes away."

My heart aches. I would give anything to fill this void for Mandy. But she must learn, as I have learned, to live with it.

"I know, Monk," I tell her. "I wish we had a daddy, too, but we don't, so we have to take care of ourselves."

Mandy nods sadly and brings her thumb up to her mouth again.

"Hey," I say, playfully swatting it away. "I

thought you were a big girl now."

"I am," says Mandy, pursing her lips.

"Good." I smile. "Then I can count on you to keep our secret about Mommy, right?"

"You mean, and go to school?"

"That's what I mean."

A small cry comes from the bedroom. Casey is waking up. Mandy still hesitates and I bend down until we are face to face. "I'm counting on you," I say quietly, "and so is Casey."

Mandy stares into my eyes a long moment, then takes a deep breath and nods. "I will do it, Anna."

6

I hurry down the road, bouncing Casey on my hip, until I get to Nate Leon's driveway. I hesitate a moment, intimidated by the fine house and wide green sweep of lawn with its expansive view of the mountains. But then Nate Leon comes out of the front door. I recognize his tall, broad-shouldered figure even without my glasses, which I have managed to leave at home, sort of accidentally on purpose.

"Hi," he calls. There is a questioning note in his voice. No doubt he is wondering what has prompted this unexpected visit.

"Hi," I answer, fidgeting with my hair, which I have accidentally on purpose forgotten to pin up, too.

As Nate comes closer I can see that he is smiling. Is it my imagination, or is he looking at me that way again? My cheeks grow warm, and I am thankful once more for my dark skin.

He stops in front of me and says out of the

clear blue sky, "You look pretty. I like your hair like that."

I'm speechless. No one has ever said such a thing to me. No one. And certainly no boy. My thoughts fly out of my head and I stand there with my heart beating to a jerky little rhythm and my tongue tied into a knot.

"Who's this?" Nate asks, giving Casey a playful poke in the ribs.

I become aware that Casey has caught hold of a hank of my flying hair and shoved it into his mouth. "Oh," I say, my voice coming out in a squeak. "This is Casey, my little brother."

"No kidding. I didn't know you had one."

I nod, gently tugging my hair loose only to have Casey grab the next piece that blows his way and shove it into his mouth.

Nate laughs. "Looks like he likes your hair, too."

I blush and laugh awkwardly. "Yeah," I say. "Now you can see why I don't wear it down."

Nate nods. "You should, though," he says. "It really looks great."

I lose my voice again and stare at the ground. Why does he keep saying these things to me? Is he serious, or is he teasing? I have so little experience with boys, I have no idea.

"So . . . why are you here?" he asks.

I look up at him, still tongue-tied.

"I mean, not that I don't appreciate the company or anything. It's just that you usually don't go out of your way to be friendly."

I feel myself stiffening. "Well," I say defensively, "people usually don't go out of their way to be friendly to me either."

Now it's Nate's turn to blush, and with his freckled skin his embarrassment is easy to see.

Casey begins to fret and wiggle in my arms.

"Anyway," I say, "you're right. This isn't a social call. I just came to ask a favor. Would you mind . . ."

"No, wait a minute," Nate interrupts. "I've tried to be friendly to you before."

"Oh, really?" I say. "When?"

Nate hesitates. "How about yesterday?" he says. "You saw me looking at you when I got off the bus, but would you look back? No. You deliberately turned away."

I'm caught, I know. His words are true and I have no defense. "Well . . ." I admit uncomfortably. "I guess I'm . . . not used to people being friendly. I just figure they must be after something."

Nate's eyes widen. "Oh, that's a great attitude," he says. "No wonder you don't have any friends."

I prickle with anger. Who does he think he is, judging me like this? He knows nothing about me. "Look," I snap, "I have reasons to have an attitude like that, and furthermore, I don't see where any of it's your business!"

Nate takes a step back. "Hey," he says, "cool down, will you? I didn't mean to make you mad."

I suddenly have no wish to continue this conversation. I shift Casey to my other hip and dig into my jeans pocket.

"My mom's sick," I say shortly, "and I have to stay home with the baby. Will you give this to the office for me?"

Nate reaches for the note. "Sure," he says.

"And, could you possibly get my homework assignments?" I hesitate. "I . . . think my mom may be sick a while."

Nate shrugs. "Sure, no problem."

"Thanks. I appreciate it." I turn and start to walk away when I remember the history test. I turn back. "About history," I say, "would you . . ." My voice breaks and I have to start over. "Would you tell Mrs. Andriadi I studied real hard. I'll . . . I'll take the test when I get back."

Nate stares at me.

"Please," I add.

He nods and I turn away once more.

"Hey," he calls.

I look over my shoulder.

"Don't be mad, okay? I'm sorry."

I nod quickly and hurry away.

By the time I get home I'm sweating and my arms ache. Small as Casey is, he can be quite an armful after a while. I put him in his playpen, then twist my hair back into a knot and put my glasses on.

Who cares what Nate Leon thinks? Who cares what any of them think! Attitude, huh! I'll show them attitude.

I slam Mandy's breakfast bowl down on the table.

"Are you mad at me, Anna?" she asks, staring up with worried eyes.

"What? Oh, no, Monk. I'm sorry. I was thinking about something else. Just eat your breakfast now, okay? We don't want to be late for the bus."

I pack her lunch box while she eats, then I pick Casey up again and walk her to the bus stop.

"I'll be here," I whisper into her ear as I kiss her good-bye. She gazes back forlornly over one shoulder as she climbs the bus steps. I watch as she slides into the front seat and pushes over to the window.

I mouth the word, "smile." With my thumb and forefinger I push my lips up into a grin. She smiles in spite of herself, then straightens up and bravely pushes her little shoulders back. I give her a wink as the bus pulls away.

Back in the kitchen, I lay Casey down in the playpen and sink down tiredly into a chair.

"Pfft," says Casey.

I look over at him. He gives me a big, toothless grin.

"What are you laughing at?" I ask. "I think I'm doing pretty good."

Casey rolls over onto his side and gets up on all fours.

"Come on," I say, smiling and motioning to him. "Keep going." He's been on the verge of crawling for a while, but he hasn't taken that first step yet. Encouraged by my attention, he giggles and rocks back and forth. A line of drool slides down his chin.

"Come on," I say. "You can do it!" I go over and crouch down in front of him. "Come on. Crawl to Anna."

He gives an excited giggle, then lifts one arm, teeters a moment, and crashes forward, right on his nose. He lets out an indignant wail.

"Oh, Casey, I'm sorry." I pick him up and hug him, trying not to laugh. "You'll get it next time. Don't worry."

The phone rings and I jump. *Mama?* I glance up at the clock. No, it's probably Mrs. Weingrad from the office at school. Casey is still sobbing and I'm glad. It will make this phone conversation more convincing. I carry him over to the phone with me.

"Hello," I say into the receiver.

"Hello, dear. Is your mother in, please?"

I recognize Mrs. Weingrad's nasal, Brooklyn accent.

"My mother is sick again, Mrs. Weingrad." I

say, holding Casey close to the phone so his cries will come across loud and clear.

"Is that you, Anna?" Mrs. Weingrad shouts.

"Yes," I shout back.

"I'm just calling to verify your absence, dear. Can I speak with your mother?"

"She's got a really bad migraine," I lie. "She says she can't even lift her head off the pillow, and the phone is way out here in the kitchen. Do you really want me to go get her?"

I can fake my mother's voice, but I'd rather not if I don't have to. I give Casey a tiny pinch and he begins to wail even harder.

"No, that's all right, dear," shouts Mrs. Weingrad. "It sounds like you've got your hands full. Just ask your mother to call when she's up to it."

"Thank you," I shout. "I'll tell her."

I hang up the phone and give Casey a hug. "Sorry about the pinch," I tell him. "I know you don't understand, but it was for your own good." I fly him around like an airplane until his sobs turn back into giggles.

"That's better," I say, holding him over my head and smiling into his eyes.

Casey purses his lips and gives me the raspberry, and I simply have to laugh.

While Casey takes his morning nap, I search through Mama's things, looking for something, anything that might give a clue as to where she's gone. As usual there is nothing, nothing but a five-dollar bill in a sweater pocket, which I snatch up like a miser and add to my stash. Another day's food assured.

When will she come home? Today? Tomorrow? The worries crowd into the front of my mind again, clamoring for control, stepping on the accelerator that makes my heart race. Slowly I force them to take a backseat, but the struggle tires me and I feel an overwhelming need to get out of this house. It doesn't matter where. Just out. When Casey wakes up, I put his hat and sweater on and belt him into his old umbrella stroller.

"It's a beautiful day," I tell him. "We might as well make the best of it." I hand him the end of his seat belt and he sticks it into his mouth and starts chewing contentedly. I pull the visor of his hat low so the sun won't bother his eyes and wheel him off down the driveway. The stroller vibrates and wobbles in the pebbly dirt, but Casey doesn't mind. The more it bumps, the more he seems to like it.

I turn out of the driveway in the opposite direction from Nate Leon's house and head up the road past Mel's Convenience Store. It feels good to be out in the sunshine and fresh air. It's cooler than yesterday, but sparkling clear and pleasant. Almost overnight the willows have leafed out, erupting here and there out of the rosy gray mountains like frothy yellow fountains. Their beauty comforts me. A mile or so down the road I come to the entrance of the Westbridge Game Preserve. That's what they call it anyway. I don't know why. It just seems like an ordinary park to me. A game preserve should have lions or elephants or giraffes in it, I think, or something a little more exciting than squirrels and birds.

I love the park, though, whatever they call it, and I turn in at the sign. The public beach part of the park isn't open yet and few people come here in off-season, especially on weekdays, so Casey and I will probably have the place to ourselves. Maybe we'll even catch a glimpse of some "gamier" game if we're quiet.

As if he has heard my thoughts, Casey begins to utter a long loud "Aaaaaa," apparently for no other reason than to hear his own voice. The jouncing of the stroller makes it come out like "Ah . . . ah . . . ah . . . ah . . . ah . . . ah . . ." and this seems to please Casey so much that he turns up the volume as loud as his little lungs will allow. I smile to myself. So much for sneaking up on wild animals.

The paved entry road ends and we reach the barrels that block access to the park in the off-season. One of them has been pushed aside and a set of rutted tire tracks curve around it. I lift the stroller over the ruts and set it down again on the other side. The ruts go off to the right, toward the lake, where the ranger's cabin is. They were probably made by his Jeep, bringing in some early season supplies. I'm not in the mood to explain why I'm here on a school day, so I push the stroller off to the left even though it will take longer to reach my destination that way. The park trails are laid out in a series of widening loops. I take the outermost one, pushing Casey farther and farther up the mountainside and deeper and deeper into the forest. At last we come to a familiar jog in the trail, and it is here that I leave the stroller, striking off into the woods with Casey on my hip. He looks around curiously.

"I'm going to show you a secret," I tell him.

He smiles as if he understands.

We make our way through a thick grove of pines. It is lovely and dark here, quiet as a cathedral, and fragrant as a Christmas tree. The needles underfoot are spongy and soft, and the walking is easy. No underbrush grows. It is a spiritual place to me, a place where I can feel some peace.

When we come out into the sunshine again on the other side of the grove we pick up another old trail and climb still higher. We are out of the park now, but I don't know who owns this land. It is part of the same ridge that stretches back behind our house. I have even found a shortcut through the woods, but it is boggy and wet this time of year.

Casey is getting heavy again, and I'm glad when we finally reach the brook. I follow its banks until we come to a broad, upward-sloping meadow.

"Look," I tell Casey, "there it is." I point up the hill to a little tumbledown log shack. Casey's gaze follows my arm only as far as my watch, which he bends over and starts gumming.

"I know it doesn't look like much," I tell him, "but it's my secret. Ours now. Nobody else knows it's here."

I carry Casey up the hill and sit him down under a tree. He immediately picks up an old dead leaf and stuffs it in his mouth.

"No, no," I say, "dirty," pulling the leaf away and offering him my watch instead. He grabs it, bangs it on the ground a couple of times, then sticks it in his mouth.

I hop up onto the cabin's old porch and walk across it gingerly. I haven't been here since last fall and I'm not sure the floorboards are still safe. They groan and creak, but tolerate my weight well enough. I give the weather-beaten door a push and peer inside, looking for signs of visitors, human or otherwise. There is a pile of tiny bones and feathers in one corner where some kind of creature has dined recently, but that's it. I frown, though, when I see the hole that has opened up in the roof over near the chimney. Once Mama gets back I will come up here and fix it somehow. I can't have my secret cabin falling apart.

I jump back down off the porch and pick Casey up, carrying him around the yard and showing him some of the relics I have found on other visits: an old bucket full of bullet holes, a white enamel basin with the bottom rusted out, a tin milk can, also full of bullet holes, and a broken shovel. He is unimpressed.

"All right," I say. "So much for the tour. Let's go sit down. My arms are tired." I take Casey up onto the porch and sit with him in a little patch of sunshine at the far end. I lean my head back against the old log wall and sigh contentedly. It's beautiful here and the view of the mountains is spectacular.

A hollow, honking cry sounds overhead, followed by another, and another. I look up and watch a flock of Canada geese go by, strung out wing to wing across the sky in a long, trailing V. I have read that they fly in formation that way because each bird creates a draft that helps pull the others along in its wake. When the lead bird tires it simply drops back and another moves up to take its place.

I sigh wistfully, wishing people were like that, willing to help each other without judging, willing to help simply because help is needed. Then again, maybe there are people like that. Maybe that's what a real family is all about.

Casey pulls the watch from his mouth and bangs it on my knee. I look down at him and smile. "What?" I ask.

He grins and stuffs the watch back in his mouth as if to say, "Nothing. Just wanted to make sure you didn't forget I was here."

"All right," I tell him with a laugh, "I'll talk to you. I'll tell you a story about the people who used to live here."

"Geee," Casey babbles.

"They were a pioneer family," I say, beginning the story I have made up for the cabin, "and they had lots and lots of children. Every day they all worked together. The girls helped their mother in the house, cooking and cleaning and sewing, and the boys worked outside with their father in the fields, planting and harvesting, and taking care of the animals."

Casey kicks his feet and chortles.

I point into the woods. "See those rock walls?" I tell Casey. "They built them. And they cleared this whole hillside. None of those smaller trees were here then. It was all pasture."

Casey takes the watch out of his mouth and stares at me. "Gah?" he says.

"Yes," I assure him. "It's true. And at the end of the day they would all wash up for dinner down there in the brook, and then, after dinner, they'd come out and sit here. There was an old rocking chair over there and the mother would sit in it and rock the baby. The father would sit on a bench right there, just under the window, and all the other kids would sprawl on the porch floor, like us, and the father would tell them stories. Would you like me to tell you one of the stories?"

Casey drops the watch and rubs his eyes, then he starts to whine and wiggle. I pick up the watch and give it back to him. He puts it in his mouth again and the whining and wiggling stop.

"One day," I begin, "in the middle of winter, Ma got a hankering for strawberries.

"'Ain't no strawberries to be found, woman,' said Pa. 'There's a foot of snow on the ground!'

"Ma kept hankering after strawberries, though, and being that she was expecting again, Pa thought it might be best to humor her. He strapped on his snowshoes and off he went. Well, the next thing you know, he came across a big ol' bear.

"'What are you doing up in the middle of winter?' asked Pa.

"'Looking for strawberries,' said the bear.

"'Now that's peculiar,' said Pa. 'I'm looking for strawberries, too.'"

Casey's weight shifts, and I look down and see that he has fallen asleep, his head resting on my arm. I tilt him back gently until he is snuggled against my chest. His face is like an angel's and I stroke his soft, pink cheek with the back of my fingers, amazed at how much I have grown to love him in the short time he has been in my life. How can Mama leave him, I wonder, even for a day?

"And each night when the stories were done," I whisper, "the mother and the father would tuck all the little children into bed and kiss them good night, one by one. And they would all fall asleep together, safe and snug and happy. . . ."

I kiss Casey's sweet face, then I tilt my head back and let the sun kiss mine.

7

I wake with a start. Casey is wiggling and fretting in my arms. At first I'm confused, but then I remember where I am. I must have fallen asleep, too. I pick up my watch from the porch floor, but the crystal is all foggy and I can't make out the time. My heart begins to race. How long have I been asleep? What if Mandy came home and found us missing? She'll be terrified. I look up worriedly at the sun. It is well past the midpoint of the sky, but by how much I'm not sure. Is it one o'clock? Two? Oh, please don't let it be three!

I grab Casey up and hurry with him back down the hill and through the woods the way we came. My heart is racing faster and faster. Even if it's not three yet, it will take us the better part of an hour to get home. How could I have let this happen? How could I betray Mandy this way? She will be so scared!

Casey is fussy and hungry, and when we reach the stroller and I belt him in he starts to scream. I don't even have a bottle for him or a dry diaper. Ranger or no, I push the stroller off toward the lake. All that matters now is getting home as fast as I can.

The stroller jounces over the rough trail, but the motion doesn't soothe Casey's hunger. He screams louder and louder and I am relieved when the lake finally comes into view. We pass the ranger's cabin and hurry on toward the wide, wooden bridge that traverses the top of the dam at the lake's near end. There is no sign of the ranger, or his Jeep. Casey is howling now.

"See the birdies?" I say in an effort to distract him. I point to the flock of Canada geese that have landed on the glassy surface of the water. Casey takes no notice.

At last we reach the bridge. *Bump, bump, bump.* The stroller thumps over the old wooden timbers. Casey's head bumps, too, and for a moment this new motion seems to draw his attention away from his hungry stomach.

"See the birdies," I try again, pointing to one that has come in close. The movement catches Casey's eye and he stares at the bird. As we near the end of the bridge, my eye catches something else, a large bright glow in the water, far below the goose, as if the sun is shining down through the water in just that one spot. I have little time to ponder it, though, because Casey's momentary curiosity has quickly given way to hunger and he renews his screaming.

We reach the edge of the bridge and I start to push the stroller along the dirt trail. It is deeply scarred here by the ruts I saw on the way in. Oddly, though, there is only one set, as if the ranger came in but did not go out again. But where is his Jeep? I look back out of curiosity, and it is then that I see that the ruts don't continue across the bridge. They veer off sharply, just before it, and disappear over the bank.

I stop in my tracks, and then the alarm goes off in my head.

I know.

As soon as the alarm goes off, I know.

With dreadful, horrible certainty, I know.

I try to push the thought away, try to deny it, as if by denying it I can somehow undo the truth of it. But I can't. The alarm is not wrong. I know.

My blood turns cold and my legs begin to tremble. Part of me wants to run, but I can't. I stand rooted, staring, needing to see, needing to prove to my mind what my heart already knows is true. I turn the stroller around and push it slowly, following the ruts back, smooth-edged ruts, not knobby, like Jeep tires would make. Smooth-edged ruts, like old, bald tires would make. Back to the embankment they lead me, then over they go and down, down to the bright glow far below in the murky water. The sunny spot. Yellow. Like Mama's car.

I'm cold. Ice cold. Shivering. Then I start to

sweat. My stomach churns and I fight the urge to vomit. My legs won't support me any longer and I sink down to my knees. I bend over holding my stomach, shaking and sweating at the same time. What's that roaring? Oh, oooh . . . I'm so sick. I rock back and forth.

Crying. Someone's crying. Casey.

I don't care. I'm so sick.

Crying harder. Casey is scared.

Breathe deep, Anna. Casey needs you. Breathe deep.

Oh, oooh. So sick. Slowly I draw in a trembling breath, slowly I let it out. Casey needs me. In and out, in and out. At last the roaring in my head dulls and I sit back on my heels, cupping my face in my shaky hands. My stomach is calming down and I can feel the strength returning to my legs. Slowly I lift my head and stare again in horror at the bright, yellow glow, long and rectangular, about the size of a station wagon.

Tears sting my eyes. "Mama?" I cry in disbelief.

I scan the embankment, looking, searching for some evidence of Mama, some sign that she got out. But there is none, and in my heart I know that there wouldn't be. Mama had to deliberately move the barrel. She had to force the old car, slipping and sliding, through the deep mud. She wasn't out for a pleasure drive.

She drove over the bank, and she never tried to get out.

The horror strikes again and I tremble all over.

"Oh, Mama . . ." I sob.

I sway for a moment, feeling faint, but Casey's desperate wailing forces its way back into my head.

Don't think, Anna. Not now. Take Casey and go home to Mandy.

Go home, Anna. Go home now.

I struggle to my feet and turn the stroller toward home.

8

I hear nothing but a loud hum in my ears as I push the stroller down the road, blindly retracing my steps. Casey is screaming somewhere out there on the periphery, but his screams can't compete with the worries that assault me, like wolves crowding in on a kill, darting in one after another to claim a piece of me and run.

What will become of me and the babies now? Who can we turn to? How will we live? Should I tell someone about Mama?

No. Not yet. Not until I can figure out what to do. But what if I don't tell? Am I breaking the law? Can they put me in jail? No, please. Not jail!

School! What will I do about school? And food! We're almost out of food. What will we do for money? And the bills! They're overdue already. . . .

Suddenly my mind goes blank. I can't think anymore. The scenery around me turns fuzzy and a numbness fills my head. My body moves mechanically down the road, until I turn in robotlike at my driveway and traverse the last few hundred feet to the front porch.

Mandy is there, huddled against the door, sobbing. I take note of her, but I feel nothing and she blends into the blur. My strength drains out of me and I can't move another step. It's as if I'm paralyzed.

After a while I become dimly aware of something moving around me. I look down and see that Mandy is kicking and flailing at me. I don't feel the blows at first, then slowly the fury in Mandy's eyes begins to register. Her shrieks of anger and betrayal make sense. Then Casey's wails penetrate, too.

I look from Mandy to Casey, from one wild-eyed, beet-red, screaming child to the other. Back and forth, back and forth, and then it begins to feel like I can't breathe. I am suffocating, drowning, the way Mama must have drowned, and Mandy and Casey are hanging on me, clutching at me, dragging me down. . . .

I bring my hands up over my face and scream, as loud as I possibly can. *"Shut up!"* I shout again, *"Just shut up! Both of you!"* God, that felt good. I stand there, hands still over my eyes, savoring the moment of silence, catching my breath. Breathing, just breathing. Okay. Better, much better. I'm going to make it now. Slowly I lower my hands. Casey has already resumed

screaming, but Mandy is staring up at me in fear
and bewilderment.

"Sorry," I am about to say, when someone
says it for me.

I whirl, and there stands Nate Leon.

"Sorry," he repeats awkwardly. "I guess I
came at a bad time."

I feel my face starting to burn.

"N-no," I stammer. "That's okay. I . . . uh,
they . . ."

"I just brought your homework," Nate interrupts. He hands me a folder with a few sheets of
paper in it. "It's all written down there."

"Thanks," I say, swallowing my embarrassment like a thick wad of gum.

I'm not usually like this, I want to tell him. *I'm
not like my mother.*

Casey is on the verge of hysteria now and I
hand the folder to Mandy and pick him up. The
welt on his forehead stands out sharply,
inflamed by all the crying.

"Is . . . are you all okay?" asks Nate.

"Yes," I say, a trifle too quickly. "Why would-
n't we be?"

Nate looks at Casey and shrugs.

"He's just hungry," I add hurriedly.

Nate nods. "I guess I'll be going then." He
turns and starts to walk away, but I can't let him
go. Not like this.

"Nate, I . . ."

He stops and looks back.

"I don't usually yell at them like that," I blurt out. "I just . . . it's just . . ."

And then I'm crying! Oh, why did I say anything at all? What an idiot I am! Now Nate is walking back toward me. Now what am I going to say?

I don't have to say anything. Nate takes Casey from my arms and smiles kindly.

"Hey," he says, "don't worry about it. I've got a couple of little brothers and sisters, too. I tell 'em to shut up all the time. Why don't you just go get his bottle while I play with him for a minute."

"Really?" I feel like I've just been thrown a life ring.

"Sure."

Casey has stopped crying just long enough to determine who is holding him. When he sees it's a stranger he registers his outrage with a loud, indignant howl. Nate laughs and shakes his head. "Just make it quick," he shouts over the screams. "I'm not a magician."

I wipe my tears away and run into the house. Mandy stomps in behind me, a suspicious scowl on her face.

"Who's he?" she demands.

I open the refrigerator and pull out the can of formula. "Just a boy from school."

"Is he your boyfriend?"

I laugh in spite of myself, glancing out through the window at Nate's handsome profile. "Of course not," I say, a bit wistfully. "I hardly know him. He just brought me my homework."

"Why's he bein' so nice then?" asks Mandy.

"I don't know. Maybe he just is nice. People can be nice, you know."

Mandy mulls this over, then lets it drop. There is a more pressing issue on her mind.

"You weren't here," she pouts. "You promised, and you weren't here."

"I know," I say gently. "I'm sorry. I just . . ." My mind darts back to the lake, but the memory jolts me like an electric shock and I quickly block it out again. "I just fell asleep," I tell Mandy. "I'm really sorry. Can you forgive me?"

"Then you yelled," Mandy goes on, obviously unwilling to consider absolution until all the sins have been named.

"I know," I admit. "I shouldn't have. It's just that Casey screamed all the way home and I was really frazzled. Please don't be mad, Mandy. I hate it when you're mad at me."

Mandy pouts a little longer, but when I reach out a hand in her direction she gives in and runs into my arms. I hug her tight.

"Thanks, monkey," I whisper. "I really needed that."

"Hey!" A shout of desperation comes from

the porch. "That bottle ready yet? This kid's going nuts!"

I run outside and rescue Nate, dropping down onto the steps with Casey in my arms. He attacks the bottle and a blessed silence ensues.

"Ah," Nate sighs, "peace." He sits down beside me. The screen door bangs and Mandy appears at our shoulders and wiggles herself down between us.

"Hey!" Nate laughs, tugging at a lock of her hair. "What do you think? I'm going to try to kiss your sister or something?"

My cheeks flush.

"Are you?" Mandy stares up at Nate, her eyes and mouth making three perfect little round O's in her face.

"I just might," says Nate, winking at me over Mandy's head, "if she wasn't so hard to get to know."

I blush even more deeply and look down at Casey. Mandy leans over and gapes up into my face.

"Are you gonna let him kiss you?" she asks.

"Shush! No!" I snap. "Of course not."

Nate laughs. "All right then," he says, giving Mandy a nudge, "ask her if maybe we can just get together and study or something?"

Mandy glares at him indignantly. "Ask her yourself," she says. "You can talk."

Nate chuckles and peers over Mandy's head.

"Okay," he says to me. "How about it?"

I look at him in bewilderment. Why is he act-ing this way? I glance away again, unsure, and the squalor around us comes sharply into focus. Doesn't this bother him—the differences in our lifestyles, our circumstances? Doesn't he realize we're not even the same color? Suddenly my eyes narrow.

"I'm black, you know," I say.

"No!" he says in mock amazement. "I thought it was a tan!"

I don't smile. "What are you trying to prove?" I ask.

Nate looks wounded. "I'm not trying to prove anything," he says quietly. "I just thought you might like a friend."

I look into his eyes and a part of me lights up inside. He's sincere. This handsome, nice, pop-ular boy actually wants to spend time with *me*, Anna. The Raggedy Anna that everyone laughs at in school. But even as I sit there pondering this wonder, a cold specter rises up inside of me. "What kind of monster are you?" the specter whispers. "How can you even think of boys at a time like this?"

A time like this. Another shock zaps me and I come to my senses. There is nothing of myself that I can share with Nate. Nothing.

"I'm sorry," I tell him. "I . . . don't have time."

Disappointment flickers in his eyes. "To study

with me?" he asks, "or to be my friend?"

I look back down into Casey's wide, blue eyes. "Either," I say quietly.

Nate stands up and shoves his hands in his pockets. "Okay then," he says, his voice cool now. "I guess I'll be going. Call me in the morning if you need me to get your homework for the vacation."

I nod without looking up, but as he walks away I watch him out of the corner of my eye.

Come back, I want to say. But instead I clench my teeth together and say nothing.

9

I move through the rest of the day in a fog. The strange hum is back in my head, and thoughts come and go in fragments, unable to organize themselves into anything that makes sense. I stare a lot, not at anything, but rather at nothing, at a fixed spot in front of me where thought does not exist. Mandy chatters incessantly and I manage to nod and mumble enough to make her think I'm listening, but I'm not. I keep busy with mindless things, folding and refolding the laundry, wiping the kitchen counter every time I walk by, sweeping and sweeping and sweeping. My hands tremble, but they do the things I ask them to do. It's as if my body knows there is a great, raw wound inside my head that needs some time to heal before I can deal with anything else.

Darkness finally comes, and the little ones are in bed. I turn to my only friends, my books, for solace, but even they can't reach me. They lay strewn across the kitchen table as I stare at the assignments Nate has written down for me.

I read the words over and over, but they will not come together, will not make sentences. There is an ache in my stomach that won't go away.

I look up at the old clock on the wall, its rusty hand marking off each second with a small, audible click. I take no notice of the time, only the motion, and the click. The only other sound in the room is the hum of the refrigerator. I feel so alone. I get up and switch on the radio, needing to hear another human voice. I look through the cupboard, not because I'm hungry, but because I think maybe food will help the ache. I push aside a box of saltines, and a jar of peanut butter, not really sure what I'm looking for. All the way in the back is a whiskey bottle I hid from Mama the other day.

The other day. Mama was still here the other day. The ache in my stomach grows.

I stare at the whiskey bottle, then my fingers reach for it. *Rare Kentucky Sippin' Whiskey,* the label says. There are a few inches of brown liquid in the bottom. I pull the cap off and sniff. My nose wrinkles up and I put the bottle on the counter and push it away. This was how Mama handled pain. She numbed herself with this until she couldn't feel anymore.

I turn away, remembering all the talk shows I've seen about children of alcoholics, all the vows I've made never to follow in Mama's footsteps. But then I turn back again. My stomach hurts so bad. Maybe . . . just this once. Just to help me get through this day.

I pick the bottle up again and tilt it to my lips. My throat burns and my eyes water as the bitter liquid slides down. I cough and gag, but then I take another sip. The liquid settles in my stomach, warm and soothing. I sink down and settle on the floor with the bottle in my hand.

I watch the clock again. Click, click, click. Every few clicks I take another sip. In time the liquid braces me, gives me the courage to think again. I allow my mind to wander back to the park, to the tire ruts, to the yellow glow. Strangely, I feel detached. No wonder Mama liked this feeling so much, this warm, floaty feeling. I take another gulp of whiskey and close my eyes.

There is so, so much to think about, so, so much to do. But for now I am tired. So, so very tired . . .

10

My head is pounding and my stomach aches. My tongue is thick and coated with a terrible-tasting fuzz, and I am dying of thirst. I open my eyes and find myself on the cold, kitchen floor. I moan and roll over, and my face bumps up against the bottle. The smell of it makes my already queasy stomach lurch. I get to my feet and dash for the bathroom. The pain in my head makes me stagger and I barely reach the toilet in time. I fling myself down and retch into the bowl over and over. My head throbs with every convulsion and I think that I have never been so sick. I wish I could die. I don't, though. I retch until there is nothing left inside of me, and then I lie there with my head on the toilet seat, not daring to move for fear that the throbbing in my head will start again.

Memories return. Mama. The lake. The yellow glow. I moan once more, so sick, body and soul. Thirst pulls me to gather my legs beneath me and push myself up. I lean over the sink and switch on the bathroom light. The glare sets my head pounding again and I close my eyes against it. I turn on the cold water, lower my face slowly and splash water all over it. I cup some in my hand and take a small sip. It is cool and sweet and I gulp some more, trying to rid my mouth of the horrible taste of bile. My stomach churns, warning me that it won't tolerate any more water. I open my eyes slowly and stare at the face in the mirror. My normally warm, brown skin is dusty gray, and the whites of my eyes are red. My hair sticks out in all directions and my lips are blue. I hate myself. How many times have I seen Mama this way, slumped over the sink, looking like hell, smelling like vomit? I will not let the babies see me this way. And I will never, never be this way again.

I flush the toilet and stagger back out to the kitchen. Every movement is torture. Every step sends a painful jolt reverberating through my head. I bend slowly and pick the whiskey bottle up off the floor. My hand shakes. If the babies weren't here I would smash this awful bottle against the wall. But they are here, so I pour it out instead, watching the last of the oily, amber liquid swirl away down the drain. I bury the bottle as deep as I can in the bottom of the trash.

"Never again," I say to myself and in my mind I hear an echo. It is Mama's voice. *Never again, Anna. Never again.*

I squeeze my hands into fists until my nails cut into my palms. "I will not be like her," I swear. "I will not!"

My stomach lurches again and I rush back to the bathroom. The water comes up and nothing more, but I keep retching anyway. I have the dry heaves. I have watched Mama suffer with them a million times. There is nothing to do but wait for them to pass. I stumble into the living room and lie down on the couch. It is two A.M. I close my eyes and pray for the nausea to go away. I must be better by morning. I must.

I lie moaning and tossing the rest of the night. Four or five more times I dash to the bathroom. I wonder how Mama could put herself through this over and over and over. I never want to feel this way again. At last, near dawn, my body rests and I appreciate what a blessing it is to be free of physical pain. My exhausted body seems to melt into the warmth of the couch and I doze. When I wake again the room is filled with light. Morning has come, the same way morning has come every day of my life. Everything has changed, and yet, nothing has changed. Life goes on.

A small sound comes from the bedroom. Casey is starting to fret. In a moment Mandy will be up, too. I push my ragged afghan aside and sit up. My head aches when I move, and I feel weak and vaguely queasy, but the worst is over. I will manage. I will put one foot in front of the other, and I will manage.

The bedroom door creaks open and Mandy pads down the hall and through the kitchen. She appears in the doorway and looks questioningly at me.

"No," I tell her, "Mommy didn't come home." She will have to be told the whole truth, I know, but not yet. Not until I have everything under control.

Mandy nods in resignation. "Casey's awake," she says.

"I know."

By the time I get to the bedroom, though, Casey is quiet again. I peek around the door, and then my heart lifts and a smile comes spontaneously to my lips. Casey's two small fists are wrapped around the crib bars, and his big blue eyes peer out at me over the side rail.

"Mandy, come see!" I call. "Casey's standing up!"

Mandy dashes to my side and together we push the door open. Casey's little head wobbles, and he looks a bit unsure as he struggles to maintain his balance.

"Casey!" I cry. "Look at you! You stood up all by yourself!"

My praise seems to convince Casey that this new achievement is a good thing, and he bursts into a happy grin.

"Good boy!" shouts Mandy, clapping her hands as if Casey is a dog who has learned a new trick. "Good Casey!"

Casey gets so excited that he starts to bounce up and down, loosing his grip and falling backward into the crib.

Mandy and I laugh, and I run over and pick him up before he has a chance to cry.

Mandy tugs at my shirt. "I wanna kiss him," she says, stretching up on tiptoes and grabbing Casey's neck.

I bend down and she gives him a big wet smack on the cheek. Casey struggles to free himself, but just before he succeeds I look at their two little faces, pressed cheek to cheek, and my eyes suddenly fill with tears.

I am so confused. I don't know what to think or where to turn. But there is one thing I do know.

"I love you guys," I whisper, hugging Casey and Mandy tight. *And I'll never let you go.*

I call Nate and ask him to pick up my assignments. His voice is cool, but his thoughtfulness still comes through.

"Are *you* sick, too?" he asks. "You sound awful."

"No," I tell him. "I just . . . didn't get much sleep last night. Will you please tell the office that I won't be back until after vacation?"

"Sure. Do you want me to find out when you can make up the exams?"

My voice sticks in my throat and I have to clear it before I can answer. "Yes, thank you," I say quickly, hanging up before I start to cry.

Mandy balks over going to school again and my promises hold little weight this time. I have to resort to bribery.

"I'm going to Mel's for more milk," I tell her, "and if you go to school like a good girl I'll get you another Sugar Daddy."

"I don't want another Sugar Daddy," she whines.

"What then? Anything you want."

Mandy's eyes widen. "Anything?"

"Well, not *anything*," I say, wishing that I could buy her something wonderful, extravagant, stupendous. Something to lessen the pain that lies ahead . . .

"Nerds?" she asks.

I nod. "Nerds it is."

Mandy still hesitates.

"And . . ." I add, "I'll rent a movie for tonight. Which one do you want?"

Mandy brightens. "*Aladdin!*" she shouts.

I shout it along with her, anticipating her choice, and we both laugh. "Okay, off you go now. Today's the last day, and then you can stay home for a whole week."

Mandy grabs her lunch box, and Casey and I

walk her to the bus stop. When the bus pulls away I shiver. The weather has turned wintry again overnight. I sigh heavily and look at Casey. "Well, Casey James," I say. "Now what do we do?"

He smiles, trusting me to think of something. Trusting me to make everything okay, the way I always do. We walk back to the house and I sit him down on the floor by my feet while I pull my sweatshirt off. My hair clip comes loose and I reach up automatically to gather my hair into a knot again, but then I pause, staring at myself in the little mirror by the door. Mama isn't here anymore. I don't have to do things her way. I hesitate a moment longer, hands in the air.

"This is you, Anna O'Dell," I hear her say. "Don't go pretendin' to be somethin' else."

Slowly I lower my hands and shake my hair loose, down around my shoulders. I take off my glasses and stare at my reflection, not far away and blurry this time, but up close and clear. Nate Leon's words come back to me. "You look pretty like that." You look pretty.

And I do, I think. I do.

"I'm not pretending, Mama," I whisper. "This is me. Can't you see? This is me!"

11

I push Casey toward the park, feeling stronger somehow with my long hair blowing in the wind. I know what I must do, at least for now. I've got to buy us some time. Soon people will start asking questions. Soon people will come looking for answers. The longer I can keep anyone from discovering the truth about Mama, the better. It will be bad enough when they find out she's disappeared. That will mean foster care again. But if they find out she isn't coming back, they'll put us up for adoption, and I know what that means. Casey will be snatched up in an instant, and probably Mandy, too, maybe even by the same family. They're beautiful, blue eyed, and blond—and young enough to be prime for adoption. But who's going to want their teenage biracial sister? No one, that's who.

The park doesn't officially open until Memorial Day, a month and a half away. It's not much time, but it's better than nothing. I've got to try and keep the yellow glow a secret until then.

When Casey and I reach the entrance, I look around to make sure no one else is in sight, then I roll the heavy barrel back into place. Once we're on the other side of the barrier I breathe a little easier. I'm still nervous, though. It feels like I'm doing something wrong, something evil. But I'm doing what I have to do. There is no choice.

I stand staring toward the lake, feeling cold and hollow inside. Dark clouds are building in the sky, turning the mountains into shrouded shadows. The surface of the lake churns in the wind, forbidding and gray.

"Ga," says Casey. He stares up at me with concern, as if he senses my fear. He reaches out, offering me a chew on his soggy seat belt.

I smile in spite of the gloom. "No thanks, honey," I tell him. "I've got work to do."

Reassured by my smile, he goes back to chewing and I begin the job of stomping down the tire ruts. The damp earth flattens easily beneath my feet, but the ruts are wide and deep and it is a long way to the lake. Casey watches birds and old brown leaves fluttering in the oak trees, and I stomp. Casey sings little tuneless baby songs while the thick clouds roll by overhead, and I stomp. Casey starts fussing and I take a break long enough to give him a bottle, then, while he fusses himself to sleep, I stomp some more. My nose is running and my back aches, my shoes are wet and my toes are numb, but slowly I close the distance to the lake. At last I'm at the edge of the embankment, looking down at the yellow glow.

It doesn't seem real today. I look at the yellow glow and feel nothing. It has no connection to my life. This is a task to be done, that's all. Still, I'm frightened. *Afraid to go on.* I have done nothing yet. Stomped on some mud, that's all. Maybe that's enough. Maybe I should go.

I look back at Casey, sound asleep, trusting in me, depending on me, and then I look again at the yellow glow. I sigh deeply. The ranger will see it. The ranger will know. I have to keep going.

I bend down, scoop up an armload of damp, soggy leaves, and walk to the bridge. As I lean out over the yellow glow I hear a sound—a twig cracking? A footstep? I turn back quickly, my heart thumping. I scan the woods and see nothing. Then the leaves rustle nearby and I see a squirrel bounding lightly up a tree. I release a shuddering breath of relief, but still, I'm afraid. What if someone does see me? What will I say? What can I say? I'm hiding my mother's body?

My mother's body.

The words pierce through me and sweat breaks out on my upper lip. God, this is hard.

Casey shifts in his stroller. He'll be awake soon. Time is running out. I run back for more leaves. Back and forth I go, flinging bunches and bunches of wet, moldy leaves into the lake.

Casey wakes up and I give him another bottle

to buy myself a little more time. He finishes this bottle, throws it on the ground and begins to arch his back and fuss. He is tired of being strapped in and undoubtedly needs changing. I throw a last load of leaves into the lake and try to spot the yellow glow. The water is so clouded with mud and silt that I can't see it. Finally the clouds overhead let loose and fat drops begin to plop into the water, dimpling the surface.

"Uh, uh, uuuhuh!" Casey fusses.

I run over, unbuckle him and pick him up. A raindrop hits him on the nose and he blinks in surprise. I kiss his cold, rosy cheek.

"You've been such a good boy," I tell him. "We're going home in a minute. Just another minute, okay?"

He wiggles unhappily in my arms and I get a whiff of dirty diaper.

"Okay," I promise, "we're going." I walk with him back to the bridge, wipe the rain from my glasses and look down one last time. The mud is clearing and here and there a patch of yellow still shows, but it's better, I think. Isn't it? I look back at the tire ruts, still plainly visible despite my hours of work, and the gloom closes in again. Who am I kidding? This will never work. This will never work! What was I thinking? Am I out of my . . .

Stop it! Just stop it, I tell myself. *You've got to be stronger than this. It will work. It will work. It will . . .*

12

"**What the? What** happened to you? And look at my floor! What on earth have you been up to?"

I stop in my tracks as Mel comes around the counter glaring at my feet. I shift Casey over to my hip and look down at my sneakers. I have left a trail of mud in my wake.

"Sorry," I mumble.

"Sorry? Is sorry gonna clean my floor? What's the matter with the doormat? Why didn't you use the doormat?"

"I did," I insist.

"Oh, right. You kids are all the same—sail right over the mat. You think it's gonna reach up and grab the dirt off your feet? You gotta wipe, I tell you. Wipe!"

I stare at Mel's angry face. *Who cares about your damn floor,* I think to myself. *My mother is dead.*

DEAD! The word reverberates through my head. I have not said it before. Have not framed it into words. Tears begin to constrict my throat and sting my nose. I lower my eyes so Mel will not see. But soon the tears are gone, and I feel numb again. I walk back and drag my feet wearily across Mel's rubber mat. Casey starts to cry.

"Happy?" I snarl as I pass under Mel's nose.

"Phew," he says. "That kid needs changing."

"I know that," I snap. I walk over to the baby food section and reach for the formula. It's awkward trying to hold Casey and carry the formula, too, but I manage to juggle two cans by stacking one on top of the other and balancing them under my chin. I start toward the register.

"Say. Where's your mother?" Mel asks suddenly.

"What?" My head jerks up, and the cans crash to the floor. One of them lands on my toe.

"Oww!" I shriek, hopping up and down in pain.

"Oh, jeez," shouts Mel, throwing his hands up in the air. He comes down the aisle and pulls Casey from my arms. "Here, here," he said. "Shush now. Look what Uncle Mel has for you." While I grab my foot, Mel pulls a box of zwiebacks off a shelf, rips it open and sticks a biscuit into Casey's open mouth. Casey is upset for a minute, then his eyes open wide, and he reaches up and grabs the sweetened bread from Mel. He pulls it out of his mouth, looks it over curiously, then reinserts it and starts gumming.

"There," said Mel. "That's better, eh?" He pulls a handkerchief out of his back pocket and dabs at Casey's eyes and nose.

"What on earth is going on out here?" asks Mel's wife, Mary, appearing from behind a curtain at the back of the room.

"She dropped a can on her toe," says Mel.

"Oh, my!" Mary hurries over. "Are you all right, dear?"

I nod. "I think so."

We all look down at my foot, then Mel groans. "My floo-or."

My dancing has loosened more mud from my sneakers and left a great, dull, brown circle on Mel's clean linoleum.

"Never mind the floor," Mary says. "Is the baby all right?"

Mel nods, but he pinches his nose with his free hand. "Sure stinks, though."

"Oh, the poor thing," says Mary. "Here, let me take him."

"What for?" asks Mel, hanging onto Casey suspiciously.

"What do you think for?" answers Mary. She peels Casey out of Mel's arms and grabs a package of diapers.

"You're not gonna open that whole new package, are you?" Mel calls after her as she disappears into the back room.

"Hush, old man," Mary calls back.

Mel shakes his head, then looks back down at his muddy floor and sighs.

"Sorry," I say again.

Mel stares at me, his brow wrinkled in thought. "Where'd you get so filthy anyway?" he asks. "And why aren't you in school?"

I look down at myself. I *am* filthy. My sneakers and jeans are full of mud, and bits of twigs and leaves cling to my jacket.

"Where's your mother?" Mel asks again before I have a chance to answer his other questions.

My mind starts to spin. Why does he keep asking that? Does he suspect something? I fight panic and struggle to keep my voice calm.

"She's sick," I say. "I took the baby for a walk in the woods so she could get some sleep, and we got caught in the rain."

"Sick, huh?" Mel nods. "I thought so. She hasn't been in for her cigarettes in a couple of days, and it's not like her to miss the lottery. It's thirteen million tonight you know."

"Oh, yeah." I begin to breathe more easily, "I'm glad you reminded me. She told me to buy a ticket."

Mel nods again as if to say he expected as much. We pick up the fallen cans, then he goes back to the counter and rings up the formula and the lottery ticket. I hate handing over the precious extra dollar, but it's worth it if it quells Mel's suspicions.

"Does she want her cigarettes, too?" asks Mel, reaching up into the rack over the register for a three-dollar pack.

"No!" I say quickly. "I mean, no thanks. She hasn't been smoking much. Upset stomach, you know. Just the lottery ticket. Oh, and these Nerds, and I want to rent *Aladdin* for tonight."

"Okay, sure."

Mary comes out of the back room with a fresh-smelling Casey in her arms. He grins when he sees me and pulls his mushy biscuit out of his mouth.

"Gee!" he says.

"Mmm, good," I agree.

He chortles happily and puts it back in.

Mel puts the formula, candy, lottery ticket, and movie into a bag.

"Hope it's nothing serious," he says.

"What?" I look at him, uncomprehending.

"Your mother's illness," he says. "I hope it's nothing serious."

"Oh." My throat goes dry. "No," I say quietly. "Nothing serious."

"Good." Mel smiles. "That's good." He picks up the box of teething biscuits and throws them into the grocery bag.

"I . . . uh, didn't bring enough money for those," I say.

Mel shrugs. "Don't worry about it."

Mary raises her eyebrows.

"What?" he says, raising his hands in a gesture of helplessness. "It was already open."

Mary smirks at him and gives me a conspiratorial wink.

"Thanks," I say to both of them as I reach out to take Casey.

"Don't mention it," says Mel. He leans across the counter. "I shouldn't tell you this," he says, "but it's kinda nice to see a little dirt on you. Maybe you're human after all, eh?"

I give him a wry smile. "Yeah," I admit, "and maybe you are, too."

13

When we round the bend in the driveway I'm momentarily surprised to see that Mama's car isn't there. And then I'm surprised at myself for being surprised. She isn't coming home. I know that. But I can't really seem to believe it. I can believe that she's not home now. But ever? Ever is a long, long time. She's just away, it seems. Somewhere else. The somewhere else that she's been so many times before.

"Hi, Anna."

I turn to face the voice. Nate Leon is standing a few steps behind me.

"I'm sorry. Did I scare you?" he asks.

"No, that's okay," I tell him. "I was just . . . thinking about something."

Nate walks up to the stroller and pats Casey on the head.

"Hi, dude," he says.

"Ga," says Casey, offering Nate a bite of his biscuit.

"No thanks, buddy," says Nate, "I'll pass."

"Ga!" Casey insists.

"Oh, okay, but just a bite," says Nate. He bends down and takes a pretend bite of the gooey nub. "Mmm, yum," he says, rubbing his stomach. "Thanks. That was great."

"Ajee," Casey coos with a satisfied grin.

Nate straightens up and gives me a wink, and I smile. It feels good having him here. Really good.

"Where've you been?" he asks. "You're a mess."

I laugh at the way Nate just comes right out and says what's on his mind. It's a refreshing quality compared to the way I've been raised, learning to keep my thoughts and feelings to myself.

"I know," I tell him. "I took the baby for a walk."

"In the rain?"

"It wasn't raining when we left."

"Well, it is now. Mind if we go up on the porch?"

"Oh, of course." I blush, feeling foolish. Nate picks up the stroller and carries it to the porch. I follow a step behind and set my grocery bag down beside it. Once we're all out of the rain, Nate looks me up and down again, a bemused expression on his face.

"What?" I ask.

"I still don't see how you got so messy taking

the baby for a walk," he says. "It's not raining dirt."

I laugh again. It feels good to laugh. I wish Nate could stay and keep me laughing all day. "It was more of a hike," I tell him, "in the woods."

"Oh?" Nate arches a brow. "I didn't know you were the outdoors type."

He's looking at me that way again, and my blood grows warm. "There's a lot you don't know about me," I say quietly.

"Oh yeah?" Nate smiles. "Well, we could fix that."

I look away, not trusting my eyes. I have come to like his teasing, and the way he looks at me, but I can't let him know.

"I said 'no' yesterday," I tell him. "Don't you understand what 'no' means?"

Nate looks up at me sheepishly. "I guess I didn't really believe you," he says.

The muscles in my jaw tighten. "Why?" I ask. "Because you can't believe a loser like me wouldn't jump at the chance to be with someone like you?"

Nate's brow wrinkles. "Of course not," he says. "What is it with you? Why are you so paranoid?"

"I'm not paranoid," I say. "It's just that . . . it doesn't add up."

"What doesn't add up?"

I look into his eyes and sense the futility of

this conversation. "Nothing," I say quietly. "It's just that I've got a lot of plans, you know, for college and stuff, and . . ." I glance at Casey, "and a lot of responsibilities. I really don't have time for anything else."

Nate looks genuinely disappointed. "Okay," he says with a sigh. "I can take a hint." He digs a folded piece of notebook paper out of his jeans and hands it over. "Your homework."

"Thanks." I open the paper and read it, grateful for the change of subject. "What about the tests?" I ask. "It doesn't say anything about the tests."

"Mr. Mellen said you can take the math test when you get back," Nate explains, "but Mrs. Andriadi said you can't make up the history test."

"What!" My mouth falls open.

Nate frowns. "Don't panic," he says. "She said you can do a paper instead. Five pages on any one of the first ten American Presidents, due the Monday we get back."

"Oh." I sigh with relief. I'll do ten pages, with illustrations. Papers are easy to get A's on.

"And she said not to forget a bibliography," Nate adds.

"A bibliography?" Reality suddenly sets in again. How am I supposed to get to the library? Who's going to watch the kids?

Library! What am I thinking of? How am I

ever going to go to school again? *Ever* . . . that awful word! I find myself dangerously close to tears.

"Anna?" Nate is watching me. "Is something wrong?"

The panic is back. I can't think. I can't answer. I stare at Nate blankly.

He looks all around, at the house, the yard, at Casey, and then at me. A suspicion is taking root in his mind. I can see it. I've got to get him to leave, fast.

"How's your mother?" he asks. "Is she still sick?"

"Yes," I blurt out. "I told you she was. You better go now. I've got to get back to her."

Nate doesn't leave. Instead he walks over to the far end of the porch and stands looking out at our empty driveway. "Your car isn't here," he says. "Now that I think about it, it wasn't here yesterday either."

I can feel the blood rushing to my head, hear it pounding in my ears.

"It's in the shop!" I snap. "If it's any of your business."

Nate turns and stares at me. "All right," he says at last. "Don't go getting all cranky again. Like I said, I can take a hint." He hops over the porch railing and drops to the ground.

"If you need anything," he says, "you know where to find me."

I watch him walk away and bitterness wells up inside me. It isn't fair. I'm fifteen years old! I should be going out on dates, having friends, having fun. Casey starts to fuss and my bitterness deepens. Instead, here I am, saddled with all these problems that Mama made!

I bend down and jerk Casey's seat belt loose, then I grab him roughly out of the stroller. I hate him right now, hate him and Mandy, too. They're nothing but millstones around my neck. Life would be so much easier without them.

"Easy! Do you hear me?" I shout, giving Casey a shake.

His eyes go wide with fear and he starts to cry. Soon I'm crying, too, tears running in great rivers down my cheeks. "I'm sorry," I hear myself repeating. "I swear I didn't mean it. I'm sorry. . . ."

Before I know it Nate is holding me, and Casey, too. "It's okay," he whispers. "Take it easy. It'll be okay."

I stiffen at first and start to pull away, but then I collapse against him and sob freely. I shouldn't, I know. Shouldn't let him get so close. But his arms around me feel so good. It's been a long time since anyone has held me. So long . . . I can't remember it at all.

14

I sit on the couch, feeding Casey his bottle. I can't stop touching him, kissing him, telling him I love him. I am so ashamed of scaring him like that, so angry at myself for losing control. I think of Nate and warmth flows into the empty, achy places inside me, tugging hard at my heart. When he left he asked me to give him a call. Give him a call. Like it was that simple. Just pick up the phone and ask him over. I long for an uncomplicated life like that, but I can't afford to think of myself. Mandy and Casey are my life and I will sacrifice anything for them, friends, fun . . . Even the chance to fall in love.

I put Casey in his playpen and start to unpack the groceries. As I fold up the bag, the lottery ticket falls out and flutters to the floor. I bend down and pick it up, staring at the numbers. What did Mel say it could be worth? Thirteen million? I smile wonderingly. Thirteen million dollars would sure solve a lot of problems.

We could buy our own house, and pay someone

to take care of us. We could . . . God, we could have anything we ever wanted. We probably couldn't *spend* thirteen million, even if we wanted to. Wow. It sure would be fun trying, though.

The front door opens and Mandy peeks in. She grins when she sees me.

"You *are* home!" she says.

"I told you I would be."

She walks in and puts her lunch box on the table. "You told me that yesterday, too," she says with a little pout, "and then you weren't."

"I know, but I also apologized and promised I'd be here today, didn't I?"

"You promised yesterday, too," says Mandy.

"I know." I sigh as I help her off with her coat. "Look, monkey," I tell her, "I know Mommy makes promises all the time and breaks them, but I'm not like that. I let you down yesterday, but it won't happen again. Do you believe me?"

Mandy nods halfheartedly.

"No, you don't," I tell her, "and I don't blame you, but I *won't* let you down again. You'll see."

Mandy's pout melts away and she lets herself be hugged, then she looks up at me. "Mommy didn't come home?" she asks.

"No." I shake my head. "Not yet."

Mandy climbs up into a kitchen chair, leans her elbows on the table and rests her chin in her hands thoughtfully. "Maybe Mommy went to get another baby," she says.

"Oh, jeez," I blurt out, "I hope not."

"Why?" asks Mandy, wide-eyed. "Don't you like Casey?"

"Of course I like Casey," I say. "I love Casey, and I love you, too, but I think there are enough of us to worry about right now."

Mandy's expression darkens. "Why are you worried, Anna?" she asks.

I remember Mama's desperate voice that morning, when I caught her with her hand raised over Casey's face. "Don't you ever tell, Anna. Not ever. Or they'll take them away from us. You hear?"

They'll take them away from us.

"Anna?"

"Huh?" Mandy is watching me, waiting. I stand up and force a smile. "I'm not worried," I say, "not really. Hey, did you forget about your Nerds?"

Mandy's expression brightens instantly.

"You remembered?" she cries.

"Of course I remembered." I go over and take the little blue box off the counter and hand it to Mandy, along with the movie.

"And *Aladdin*, too!" she cries. "Can I watch it right now?"

"Don't you want to wait until after dinner?"

Mandy grins. "I'll watch it now," she says, "and after dinner, too!"

* * *

I sit perched on the edge of the couch, staring at the TV screen, the lottery ticket in my hand.

"Please, please, please," I whisper. "Please, God. I know you're not supposed to pray for money. But this is an emergency. . . ."

"And tonight's thirteen million-dollar winning numbers . . . are . . ." the announcer blares. One little tennis ball pops up into the top of the lottery machine.

"Six. Please God. Six."

"Eighteen!"

My heart sinks. I quickly scan the other numbers on my ticket. No eighteen anywhere. I listen as the other numbers are read off. Not a single match. Not one.

I crumple up the ticket, squeezing so tight that the knuckles on my hand turn white, then I drop it on the floor and stomp on it. I flop back on the couch, angry with myself for being such a fool, for pinning my hopes on anything so dumb.

I don't need anything, I tell myself. Anything or anyone, except Mandy and Casey . . . Another name forces its way into my head, and for a moment I close my eyes and remember the feeling of Nate's arms around me. He seems so kind, so caring. Maybe I can trust him.

No! I remind myself sharply. There is no safety. Not for the O'Dells. I can't trust anyone. Not for a moment.

15

April vacation seems to evaporate before my eyes, like morning mist in the mountains, the hours swept away by the busy-ness of tending to Mandy and Casey. Each morning I think, "Today I will come up with a plan." Each night, in exhaustion, I promise myself, "Tomorrow." My undone history paper weighs heavily on my mind, a silly thing to worry about under the circumstances, I know. But it's a worry I can fathom, so I cling to it, allowing it to push out the other, incomprehensible ones.

For all the worries, though, there is also a strange new peace in the house. Casey still cries and Mandy is as petulant and demanding as ever, but I don't have to look over my shoulder anymore, gauging Mama's mood, trying to restore calm before her temper hits the boiling point. My teeth are no longer clenched, the muscles in my back no longer knotted. The tension I've lived with for so many years is draining away. I can't believe that what I'm feeling is relief, relief that my mother is dead. What kind of heartless beast am I, I wonder, to feel this way?

As the end of the week draws near I lie awake longer and longer each night, thinking about our plight from every angle, thinking until my head grows heavy from the weight of it all. No answers come to me. When Mandy walks into the kitchen on Friday morning, I'm sinking into despair.

"Mommy's still not home, Anna," she says quietly.

I turn from the sink and look into her worried eyes. "I know," I say, and this time my facade crumbles and my voice breaks. Our money is almost gone. Mel at the store is asking more and more questions about Mama's illness, and vacation week is at an end. Time is running out.

"Is Mommy coming home, Anna?" Mandy asks straight out.

I sag back against the sink, unable to pretend anymore. "I . . . don't know," I say softly.

Mandy stares at me for a long time, then comes over and slips her arm around my waist.

"Don't worry," she tells me. "We're doin' okay."

I smile sadly. "Yeah, I know."

"Maybe Mommy *will* come home," she says, her eyes brightening, "maybe today." She is doing her best to bolster my spirits, I know, and her courage gives me strength.

"Maybe." I nod.

"Or maybe she'll write us a letter or something."

"A letter?"

"Yeah."

I put my hand to my mouth. "Letters! I forgot all about the mail. The postman will wonder why it's piling up!" I grab my jacket and dash out the door.

The leaky old mailbox is clogged with bills and advertisements, soggy and matted together from the previous day's rain. I cradle the damp mess in my arms and hurry back to the house. I dump it all on the kitchen table and Mandy watches me as I pick through and separate the catalogs, flyers, and bills.

"Anything from Mommy?" she asks.

I look into her little blue eyes, full of hope.

"No, honey. I'm sorry."

Her shoulders sag and she turns away from the table. "I guess I'll go watch TV," she says.

I sort through the letters. Electric bill—final notice. Telephone bill, too. Well, what does it matter? We can't stay here much longer anyway. When I don't show up for school on Monday they'll come looking. We have to be gone by then. But gone where?

I hold up one of the letters in the pile and

look at it. It is different from the rest. The address is hand printed and the envelope is blue. It doesn't look like a bill. The ink is badly smudged from the rain, but I can make out that it is addressed to my mother, Suzanne O'Dell. The return address is smudged, too. All I can read is Sunnydale, Mississippi. *Mississippi?* I stare at it wide-eyed. Mama was from Mississippi, though she never would say from where. Maybe there is some family, after all! Who else would be writing to Mama from Mississippi?

I start to slide my finger under the flap but then I stop. It seems wrong somehow, opening Mama's mail. It is Mama's after all. Maybe I should wait. Another day maybe, or two?

Wait for what, Anna? Wait for what?

Mandy pads back out into the kitchen. "Casey's awake," she says.

"Okay, I'll be right there."

"What's that?"

"A letter."

"For you?"

"No, for Mommy."

"Then why are you opening it?"

"I uh, thought it might be important."

"Mommy might get mad."

"I don't think Mommy cares, Mandy."

A look passes between us and Mandy says nothing more.

I slide my finger the rest of the way along the flap, fold it back and peer inside. "Oh, my God," I whisper.

"What is it?" cries Mandy. "What's in there?"

"A miracle," I answer. "There's a miracle in here!" I reach a trembling hand into the envelope and pull out two bills.

"Two dollars?" says Mandy.

"Two *hundred* dollars," I tell her.

"Wow."

"Yeah. Wow is right."

"Who sent it to us?"

I look into the envelope for a note of some sort, but there is none. "I don't know." Mandy and I stare at each other, then Mandy's eyes light up.

"Maybe it's a daddy!" she cries.

A daddy?

I turn the envelope over in my hand and examine the writing. Did my father write those words? Did his hand touch these bills I'm holding now?

Oh, please God, yes. Let the answer be yes.

If he did . . . If he is sending money, then he must care. And if he cares, then there is a chance . . .

"Do you think it is?" Mandy cries, jumping around in excitement. "Do you think it's from a daddy?"

"I don't know, Monk," I whisper, my voice

shaky, "but I'm sure going to try and find out."

"How?" asks Mandy.

"I don't know," I tell her. "We have to be real careful. I need time to think. But for now . . ." I hold up one of the bills and smile. "We're going shopping!"

16

My heart is racing and my head throbs. I lower two heavy bags of groceries onto the kitchen table, then hold the door open while Mandy pushes the stroller in, huffing and puffing.

"What's wrong, Anna?" she asks. "Why did we have to walk so fast?"

I close the door, peer out the window at the driveway, and pull down the shade. "We've got to get out of here," I tell Mandy.

"What?" She looks terrified.

"We have to go, Mandy. Mel is asking too many questions. I know he's suspicious. He may be calling the police this very minute."

"But where?" cries Mandy. "Where are we going?"

"There's a place in the woods. An old cabin. I go there all the time. We can hide there until we can figure out what to do."

Tears well up in Mandy's eyes and spill down her cheeks. "I don't wanna go, Anna," she sobs. "I'm scared." I pull Mandy over and hug her.

"Don't cry, monkey," I plead. "You'll get Casey all worried."

Mandy buries her head in my neck and twists a lock of my hair around her finger. "But I'm scared, Anna," she gasps between sobs. "I want Mommy to come ho-ooome."

The word "home" trails off forlornly. I close my eyes and struggle to stay calm myself. "I know, baby," I whisper. "I do, too. But we can't wait any longer. Don't be scared, now. It'll be fun, like camping. Just for a few days."

Mandy doesn't answer. She keeps on crying and I lower myself to the floor and rock her until she is all cried out.

"You okay now?" I ask her.

She shrugs tiredly.

I tilt her face up and look into her eyes. "You have to be okay," I say, a bit more firmly. "I need your help, and I need you to be brave."

Mandy returns my forthright gaze. "All right, Anna," she says softly.

I kiss her nose. "Good girl. Hop up now so I can put Casey down for a nap."

Mandy gets to her feet slowly, like a little old woman, and I rise and put Casey in his crib.

"Okay," I tell Mandy when I come back. "I need you to go pack your backpack with as many warm clothes as you can fit."

Mandy starts to shuffle off, but I take her hand and pull her back.

"We're going to be okay," I tell her. "I promise."

Mandy looks up at me and nods, but I can see the doubt in her eyes. And there is nothing I can do, nothing I can say, to take the doubt away.

My old duffel bag is packed with everything we'll need for the night—food, blankets, diapers, and a few cooking utensils. I fill my backpack with clothes. I will sneak back tomorrow to get more supplies. For now we have all we can handle. Mandy and I slip into our boots and I strap Casey to my chest in his Snuggli carrier. I sling the duffel over my shoulder and give Mandy both backpacks, one to wear and one to carry.

"This is going to be fun," I reassure her as we make our way across the backyard and into the woods. We will take the shortcut, even though it will be hard going. We can't chance being seen on the road.

Mandy gives me a dubious, sidelong look. "What if Mommy comes home while we're gone?" she asks.

"Don't worry. I'll check back every day," I tell her. "If Mommy comes home, I'll know."

It is a chilly day, but soon we are sweating under our burdens. After a half hour or so

Mandy sits down in a heap. "How far is this?" she grumbles. "I'm tired."

"Not much farther, Monk. You're doing real good."

After a short rest I get her to her feet again and we plod on. The going is swampy now, and progress is slow, but finally, after several more rest stops, and a snack break, we reach the brook below the cabin.

"Here we are," I say. "Home sweet home."

Mandy stares disdainfully at the tumbledown shack. "That's it?" she says.

"Yeah. Isn't it neat?"

"The roof is falling down."

"Just in one corner. I can fix it."

"With what?"

"Never mind. That's not important now. Let's just go up and get unpacked."

I break off a pine bough and use it to sweep the dry leaves and debris out of the cabin, then I spread one of the blankets and sit Casey in the middle of it. I hand him his keys and he shakes them happily and puts them in his mouth.

"See," I tell Mandy, "Casey likes it here."

She stands sullenly in the middle of the room, taking stock of her surroundings.

"Where's the kitchen?" she asks.

"There isn't one. You cook in the fireplace."

"What about the frigerator?"

"There isn't one of those either, but we can keep things cold in the brook."

Mandy glances around once more. "Where do you go potty?"

"In the woods."

"In the woods!"

"Of course. What do you think you do when you're camping?"

Mandy crosses her arms over her chest. "I wanna go home," she announces.

"We are *not* going home," I say.

"I wanna."

"No."

"Yes!" Mandy stamps her foot, then turns and runs for the door. I dart after her, catching hold of her out on the porch.

"Let me go! I wanna go home!" Mandy kicks and thrashes, trying to break free of my grasp. "I wanna go. Mommy might be home now. Mommy might be . . ."

"Mandy!" I clap a hand over Mandy's mouth. "Stop that screaming. What if someone's nearby? What if they hear?"

Mandy twists her head free. "I don't care. I wanna go *home*! Mom-meee! Mommy, Mommy, Mom . . ."

"Stop it!" I grab her by both arms and give her a shake. "Stop it, you hear?"

Mandy stops and instinctively brings her hands up to protect her face. I am startled by the gesture. I let go of her arms, ashamed.

"Mandy," I say gently, "I would never hit you. Don't you know that?"

Mandy lowers her hands and peers up at me.

"I want to go home," she says softly. "I want Mommy."

I sigh. Taking Mandy's hand I lead her back into the cabin. I sit down on the blanket next to Casey and pull her into my lap. The time has come. Mandy must be told.

"We can't go home, Mandy," I say gently. "Mommy isn't there. Mommy isn't coming back."

Mandy straightens in my lap and twists her head to look up at me. "How do you know?"

"Because . . . Mommy's in Heaven now."

"Wh-what?" Mandy's eyes go wide.

"I didn't want to tell you yet. Not until I had everything figured out. But you need to understand."

Mandy settles back into my arms and puts her thumb in her mouth. Her eyes go glassy and she starts to hum the Mr. Roger's theme song, "It's a Beautiful Day in the Neighborhood." It's her comfort song. She hums it to herself after beatings, curled up in a corner, nursing her bruises. There are never any tears, not in front of Mama. Tears make the beatings worse. Only humming.

I stroke her hair and let her hum, let her take her time. Casey tosses his keys aside, leans over my leg and pats Mandy's head, too. In time the thumb comes out, and Mandy grabs Casey and hugs him tight. Casey tolerates the hug for a minute or two, then struggles until Mandy lets him free. She looks up at me then, her eyes clear again. "How do you know, Anna?" she asks.

"About Mommy?"

She nods.

"I . . . I'd rather not tell you that, Monk. It's not important anyway. What's important is that we all stick together. We're all we've got left now."

Mandy brings her thumb back to her mouth and lays her head against my shoulder once more. "Look!" she says suddenly.

I look where she's pointing. Casey is up on all fours, rocking back and forth, his gaze firmly fixed on his keys, several feet ahead. I smile down at Mandy, touching a finger to my lips to warn her to be quiet. We watch in silence as Casey lifts his hand, moves it forward and down again, then follows with his knee. The other hand, the other knee, and he is moving slowly, steadily toward his goal. At last he grabs the keys and sinks to the floor again, kicking his feet like a happy little frog.

"Yay!" I shout, clapping my hands.

"Yay, Casey," Mandy echoes, scrambling over and looking earnestly into Casey's face. "You crawled!"

I lean over and scoop Casey up, planting a kiss on his cheek. "What a big boy you're getting to be, Casey James," I whisper. I turn and smile over at Mandy, but Mandy's smile is gone. Instead, a little tear glistens in the corner of her eye.

"What is it, Monk?" I ask, reaching out to her.

She doesn't move. "Who's going to take care of us now?" she asks in a trembly voice.

I reach for her hand and pull her close.

"I'll find someone," I promise. "Don't you worry. All I need is a little more time."

I lie in the darkness, listening to the strange rustlings of the night creatures. Little clicking footsteps crisscross the roof. A short while ago two raccoons had a fight under the cabin, hissing and screaming in horrible, humanlike voices that sent chills up my spine. The stars shine down through the hole in the roof. The moon is out, too, somewhere beyond my view. It casts eerie shadows on the cabin wall. I'm feeling small and scared. Telling Mandy about Mama has made it real, made me realize that I'm it, the oldest in my family, the end of the line. Mama was never much security, but she was something, the anchor to which we moored our flimsy little lifeboat. Now we are cut free and drifting, and I am all alone in the universe. All alone except for these two little bumps in the blanket, huddling close to me. I am their anchor now, but the universe is so very big, and I am so very small. How long can I hold on?

I reach into my backpack and touch the blue envelope with the money in it. I take it out now and hold it in my hand, gazing at the smudgy handwriting. I feel better, if just a little. It is a thin thread, a very thin thread, but for the moment it's something to cling to.

17

Morning dawns bright and sunny, unseasonably warm for April. It is a gem of a day, a gift I badly need. I draw new energy from it, like all the other living things around me. The forest is swelling with life. Even the mountains have lost their grayish tinge and grown downy with color, muted reds and yellows, pale greens and lacy whites.

"Wait until you see what I made for you," I tell Mandy as I carry in a new load of wood for our fire. Mandy sits by the chimney, tipping Casey's bottle up for him so he can suck the last few drops.

"Is it a toy?" she asks.

"No."

"Something to eat?"

"Wrong again."

"What then?"

"Come and see."

I lift Casey and Mandy jumps up and follows us outside. I lead her down a little path away from the cabin, then push aside a low hanging pine bough. There sits the old bullet-riddled milk can. With the broken shovel I have dug a hole and set it into the ground. Upside-down on top I've placed the white basin with the rusted-out hole in the bottom, banging all the sharp edges under so the basin is firmly hooked to the top of the milk can.

Mandy frowns. "What is it?" she asks.

"It's a potty."

Mandy wrinkles up her nose.

"You don't look very excited," I say.

She puts a hand on her hip and cocks her head at me.

"You expect me to get excited about a potty?" she says.

I laugh. "You used to," I tease her. "Remember when you were two? You'd carry your little potty out into the kitchen and . . ."

"Annn-na!"

"What?"

Mandy rolls her eyes. "Do you *mind*? I'd *rather* not talk about it!"

I smile. "Oh," I say, "sorry. I didn't realize you'd gotten so sensitive."

"Jeez." Mandy turns on her heel and marches back up toward the cabin.

"Hey," I call after her, "don't you want to go?"

Mandy looks over her shoulder and grimaces. "Not with you standin' there. You might take a pitchur!"

* * *

I spend the rest of the morning cleaning out the cabin and gathering kindling and firewood. For the first time since Mama's disappearance I feel something close to happiness. The breeze is soft and the air as sweet as a fresh-peeled ear of corn. Even Mandy is content looking for tadpoles down by the brook. If I don't think too hard, I can almost let myself believe that we're going to be okay, that we can make it here in this little cabin.

We have lunch and I put Casey down for his nap.

"Okay, Mandy," I say, tossing the empty duffel over my shoulder. "I've got to go to the house now and get some more stuff."

Mandy jumps up and clutches my hand. "I wanna come."

"You can't come," I tell her. "You have to stay with Casey."

"Let's bring him," she says.

I bend down and put a hand on her shoulder. "Mandy," I say firmly. "I can't take you and Casey. I need to be able to go fast and carry as much stuff as I can."

She looks around apprehensively. "But I'm scared to stay here alone," she says. "What if a bear comes?"

I smile. "You're not alone. You're with Casey."

"He's no help."

"Sure he is. You should see him when he gets mad. He stands up big and tall—almost two feet tall! And puts his fists up and shows his teeth and growls."

Mandy starts to smile. "He does not."

"He does! Why, any self-respecting bear would run for the hills."

Mandy grins and shakes her head. "You're full of baloney, Anna," she says. "He hardly even has any teeth."

I laugh. "Yeah, I know. But he's got some really strong gums!" I give Mandy a wink. "You'll be fine, Monk, honest. I won't be gone long and I'll bring some storybooks back, and then later we'll read and play games, okay?"

"What kind of games?" asks Mandy.

"Oh . . . hide-and-seek, and charades."

"Okay," Mandy agrees reluctantly.

As I pull the door shut behind me, I can hear her start to hum "It's a Beautiful Day in the Neighborhood."

18

I rummage through Mama's things one last time, looking for something, anything that will give a clue to the past, a clue to the source of the mysterious blue envelope. There is nothing. Not a photograph, not a note. Nothing. How could anyone dispose of the past so thoroughly? I wonder. What was it back there that Mama was running away from, trying so hard to forget?

There isn't much time to ponder this, though. I must get back. I fill the duffel near bursting and grab a couple more blankets. As I'm about to leave I realize that I have nothing to remember Mama by, not even a photograph. My eyes fall upon her old silver-handled hairbrush, lying on the dresser. I remember sitting at the foot of the bed, watching Mama slide it through her long, golden hair, back when there was only Mama and me. I pick it up and turn it in my hand, remembering the feel of it, whispery soft against my scalp, and the feel of Mama's hands, cool and quick, taming my wild mane into neat little braids. Mama and me. I catch a glimpse of someone in the mirror, someone with tears in her eyes. It is me, though it seems like someone else. I wipe the tears away, then I shove the brush into the duffel. The babies are waiting. I hurry out the door.

I am sweating by the time I reach the brook and my arms ache. I stop a minute to catch my breath and rest. The cabin looks quiet, so I take my glasses off, kneel down, and splash cool water on my face. It is icy and refreshing and I cup some in my hands and take a drink.

As I settle my glasses on my nose again I catch sight of something up on the porch that I didn't notice before, a bundle of some sort. I squint in the sun, trying to make out what it is. It is a knapsack, a big one, the kind hikers carry—and it's not one of ours.

I splash through the brook and sprint up the hill, my heart racing. I grab a large, clublike stick, leap up onto the porch and push open the door.

"*Hey!* Take it easy!"

Nate Leon backs away from me, his hands raised in front of him. Mandy and Casey watch us from their blanket in the corner.

"Nate?" My breath comes out in a whoosh. I lower the club and stand there, just breathing. "Nate. Thank God."

Nate lowers his hands and takes a step toward me, but I suddenly lift the club again.

"What a minute," I say. "What are you doing here?"

Nate backs up. "What am *I* doing here?" he asks. "The question is what are *you* doing here? This is *my* grandfather's cabin. I camp here all the time."

I lower the club once more.

"Your grandfather's?"

"Yeah. Now, will you put that thing down? You're making me nervous."

I drop the club to the ground. "Your grandfather really owns this place?" I ask.

"Yeah." Nate nods. "My great-grandfather used to own the lake, and all the land the park is on, too, but he had to sell a lot of it off during the Depression."

Mandy runs over and grabs my hand. "He scared us, Anna," she cries.

I put an arm around her shoulders and frown at Nate.

He shrugs his shoulders apologetically. "I didn't mean to scare them," he says. "Who knew they were here? I just walked through the door and she started screaming and then the baby woke up and started crying. I just got them calmed down a couple of minutes ago."

I pat Mandy's shoulder. "It's all right," I tell

her. "Nate doesn't mean any harm. Why don't you go give Casey his juice."

"What juice?" asks Mandy.

"The juice I . . . oh, I guess I left it down by the brook. I'll go get it." I turn toward the door.

"Wait a minute," says Nate.

I turn back.

Nate cocks his head. "We know what I'm doing here," he says, "but we still don't know what you're doing here."

I can feel my face growing warm. I glance at Mandy, then back at Nate.

"We're, uh . . . camping, too."

Nate arches an eyebrow and looks over at Casey. "Camping?" he says. "With a baby?"

My face is growing hotter. "Sure," I say shortly. "Why not? The Indians did it, didn't they?"

Nate looks at me skeptically. "My mother'd never let me take my baby brother up here," he says.

I snort. "Yeah," I say. "Well, my mother's a little different than most."

I start for the door again when Nate steps forward and grabs my sleeve. "Where *is* your mother?" he asks.

I pull my arm away. "What business is it of yours?"

"You're staying in my cabin," says Nate. "I guess that makes it my business."

I stare at him angrily. This complicates

things, complicates them a lot. I'll have to tell him something to get him off my back, but I'm sure not going to tell him everything. I need time to think things through, to choose my words carefully.

"Okay," I say at last. "We'll talk, but not now, okay?" I incline my head just slightly in Mandy's direction, and Nate picks up my meaning. He nods.

"All right," he said. "Later then."

I start out the door once more.

"Need a hand?" he asks.

"Sure. Why not?"

Out on the porch I stub my foot into another bundle and nearly trip. I look down. "You brought a sleeping bag?" I say.

"Yeah. I told you, I'm camping here tonight."

I look up. "Still?"

A mischievous grin spreads across Nate's face. "Yeah," he says. "Why? Does that bother you?"

A flush creeps up my neck and warms my cheeks. "Of course not," I say, "as long as you stay on your side of the cabin."

Nate's grin broadens. "They're all my sides of the cabin," he says.

I have managed to put off answering Nate's questions all day, but now the babies are asleep and I'm out of excuses. I walk out onto the porch and sit down a few feet away from him. I take off my glasses and rub my eyes tiredly, then I put them back on.

Nate is staring at the sunset. The clouds that hang over the mountains are all pink and blue, like a baby's blanket, and the ones closest to the peaks seemed to be edged in glowing satin.

"Beautiful, huh?" I say.

Nate nods. "The most beautiful spot in the world," he says. There is an odd note of sadness in his voice and I turn to look at him, but he has turned away and is rummaging in his backpack.

"Soda?" he asks, reaching into his pack and drawing out two cans of Coke.

"Sure. Thanks." I lean back and look up at the deepening sky. It doesn't seem so big and lonely tonight. The balmy weather has lasted into the evening and the air echoes with the shrill chirps of thousands of spring peepers.

"Nice night, huh?" Nate says.

"Yeah. Awesome. Makes me feel almost like . . ."

"Like what?"

"Oh, nothing. You'll laugh."

"No I won't, honest. Makes you feel like what?"

"A pioneer."

Nate smiles. "A pioneer?"

"Yeah. You know, like the people who must have lived in this cabin once, the first settlers.

It's funny to think that it's almost the same now as it was then. All around, the world has changed, but right here, in this little clearing, it's like time has stood still."

Nate pops the top of his Coke and nods thoughtfully. "Yeah," he said, "that is kind of neat, except for one thing."

"What?"

"There weren't any early settlers here. My great-grandfather built this place as a hunting camp."

"A hunting camp?"

"Yeah."

"You mean a place where men go to smoke and drink and kill defenseless animals!"

"Well, I guess that's one way to look at it."

I frown and look around. "So are you the one who shot everything around here full of holes?"

Nate's face flushes a deep red. He looks down and slowly twirls his Coke can. "No, that happened a long time ago," he says quietly. "I don't own a gun."

"Well, thank goodness for that at least," I snap. "I hate guns." I look around again and all of my warm, pioneer dreams evaporate in an ugly cloud of gunsmoke. I sigh wearily.

"What's wrong?"

I shake my head. "Nothing. You wouldn't understand."

Nate seems just as happy to let the subject

drop. "Do you want to tell me about your mother now?" he asks.

I pop the top of my Coke and take a sip, then I draw up my knees and lock my arms around them. "She ran off," I say.

Nate doesn't say anything, but nods as if to say he'd guessed as much.

"She's done it before," I continue matter-of-factly. "She'll be back."

"Have you told anyone?" Nate asks.

"No." I shoot him a warning glance. "There's no one to tell. Besides, I can manage just fine."

Nate returns my stare for a long moment, then takes a sip of his Coke. "But she's been gone over a week," he says quietly.

"So?"

"Is she usually gone that long?"

I don't answer.

"What if she doesn't come back?"

My jaw muscles tighten. "She'll be back."

"How do you know?"

"I just know. Okay?"

Nate takes another swig of Coke and looks up at the moon, hanging like a ghostly lantern in the evening sky. We both stare at it in silence for a while, then he turns to me again.

"What about school?" he asks.

A lump rises in my throat. "I'll be back," I say hoarsely, "as soon as I can."

Nate puts his Coke down and slides over

closer to me. "Anna, this is crazy," he says. "You can't stay here."

My body tenses. "Why not?"

"Because you can't, that's all. There are a million reasons. You're not thinking straight, or you wouldn't even be trying it."

I glare into Nate's eyes. "I'm thinking just fine," I snap. "I'd like to see you come up with a better idea."

"I've got a better idea," Nate says. "Come home with me."

"Oh, right." I nod. "Your mother needs three more kids."

"She'd get you some help," says Nate.

"I don't need any help."

"Anna, you do."

I bang my Coke can down on the porch floor and a spray of Coke spurts up into my face, fueling my already hot temper.

"You listen to me, Nate Leon," I snarl. "I don't need anybody. Do you hear? I've been mother and father to those two little kids in there since they were born. They mean more to me than anything, more than school, more than friends, more than life if you want to know the truth. Nobody is going to take them away from me. Nobody. Do you understand?"

Nate pulls back. "Hey," he says, "take it easy. Nobody's trying to take them away from you." He leans over and grabs his pack and pulls out a towel. "Here," he says gently. "You've got Coke all over your face."

My shoulders sag and the venom goes out of me. I take the towel and wipe my face.

Nate shakes his head thoughtfully. "Phew," he says. "I never knew. I mean, I never guessed there was anything wrong until last week."

"Yeah, well . . . I'm a pretty good actress."

"I guess." Nate takes the towel from me and dabs at my nose. "You missed some," he said.

I smile. "Thanks."

"Look, Anna," Nate begins again, hesitantly, "what makes you think they'd split you guys up? I mean, don't they try to keep kids from the same family together?"

I sigh tiredly and lean my head back against the cabin. "Be real, Nate, will you?" I say. "How many people are out there with room in their lives for three kids?"

"I don't know. Not a lot, I guess, but maybe some."

I shake my head. "I can't take the chance."

"So what are you going to do?"

"I don't know. I'll think of something."

"I wish you'd let me help."

"I will."

"You will?"

"Yeah. You can help by keeping quiet, and maybe . . ."

"Maybe what?"

"Maybe help me fix the roof tomorrow?"

Nate smiles grudgingly. "All right," he says. "I've been meaning to do it anyway. I've got the stuff in my garage. I'll go get it in the morning."

I lean over and touch his hand. "But you've got to promise me, Nate," I plead, "that you won't tell anyone."

Nate looks down at my hand, then he turns his over and captures mine, caressing my fingers with his. "Okay," he says, looking up again, "we'll try it your way, for a while anyway."

My hand glows warm in Nate's. Our faces are so close. We stare into each other's eyes a long moment and then our lips touch.

It isn't anything like the bathroom mirror, or Clark, the teddy bear. It is soft as velvet and sweet as wild strawberries warmed by the sun. Nate pulls me close and the kiss gets deeper, sweeter. I want to get lost in it, but I dare not. I pull away breathlessly, surprised at how strongly my body resists letting go.

"No," I say. "Don't."

"Don't what?" asks Nate.

"You know what. I can't do this. I'm afraid."

"Afraid of what?"

"Of everything. Of you and me. Alone like this. My life is complicated enough already, Nate."

Nate touches a finger to my lips. "Hey," he says, "it's okay. Believe me. I'm not ready for anything complicated either. It's just a kiss. Okay?"

He smiles and I feel safe.

"Okay," I whisper.

He reaches up and gently lifts my glasses from my face, then he pulls me close and presses his lips to mine once more.

The roof is fixed, a new supply of firewood is cut and stacked under the house, and Nate is heading home. Home. How I envy him. We stand at the foot of the porch stairs, saying good-bye.

"What do I tell them in school tomorrow?" he asks.

"Nothing. You haven't seen me. You don't know anything."

Nate shakes his head. "You're kidding yourself. You know that, don't you? This won't work."

I block his words out, pretend I can't hear.

He sighs and shrugs. "Okay," he says, "we'll try it for a few days. I'll keep checking on you."

"No." I shake my head firmly. "They'll be looking for us. You can't come back here. Someone might get suspicious."

Nate stares at me a long time. "In case you haven't figured it out yet, I care about you, Anna," he says. "How do you expect me to go home and forget you're out here?"

Joy sweeps over me. I care about him, too, more than I ever wanted to. But when you care about people, you have to worry about losing them, and I can't afford to worry about anyone else. Besides, Nate knows too much already. I can't let him keep coming around, can't risk his finding out more.

I swallow hard and look into Nate's waiting eyes. "Don't care about me, Nate," I say as gently as I can. "I told you from the beginning, I don't want you in my life."

Nate winces and I hate myself for hurting him, but there is no other way.

"What?" he says. "What about last night?"

I hesitate for a moment, and then, as if on cue, Casey starts to cry and Mandy comes to the cabin door to tell me he's awake.

"I'm coming," I tell her, "just give him his bottle." Mandy disappears inside again and I turn back to Nate. "Last night was . . . just a kiss," I tell him. "Nothing more. You said so yourself. Let's leave it at that, okay?"

Nate's eyes probe mine, searching for the truth, and I fight to keep my face a blank. I'm good at it. I've had plenty of practice hiding my feelings, but this is hard. I am hurting Nate, and I don't want to.

Nate stares at me a moment longer then shakes his head. "Fine," he snaps. "You want me out of your life? I'm out. Good-bye and good luck!"

He whirls and strides away and I whirl, too,

and run up the steps, past Mandy and into the cabin.

"What's wrong, Anna?" she asks, standing wide-eyed in the open doorway.

"Nothing!"

"Then why are you crying?"

"I'm not crying!" I shout. "Just shut the damn door and leave me alone."

19

Night is falling as I stand in the cabin window, staring. If it weren't so cold I would go out there and stand in the rain, stand there and cry and cry and let the rain hide my tears. Three days have passed since Nate left, and all his dire predictions of failure are coming true. Life in the cabin is far from idyllic. Mandy and Casey and I are all beginning to sniffle and sneeze. Our clothes are dirty and so are we because it's been too cold to go down to the brook and wash. Casey has developed a diaper rash, and Mandy is constipated because she hates to use the toilet.

I can't pretend any longer that things are going to work out. We are running out of food and still I have no ideas. All I have is the mysterious envelope and a hundred and sixty dollars. I have to find out who sent the envelope and why. But the question is, how? I could take a bus down there maybe, but that would probably use up the rest of the money, and what do I do if it turns out to be a wild-goose chase? And what do I do with Mandy and Casey in the meantime?

Questions. Questions. Questions. And not one single answer. And to make matters worse, I can't get Nate out of my mind. The harder I try to forget him, the more I think about him. I long for an escape from all this turmoil. I don't want to feel. I don't want to think. I don't want to worry anymore.

"Anna?"

"Huh? Oh, what is it, Mandy? I thought you were asleep."

"My tummy hurts."

I frown, not in the mood for another problem. "It's your own fault," I say tersely. "I told you, you have to use the potty more often."

"But I don't like to," Mandy whines. "It smells bad, and it has flies."

"I don't care. It's all we've got."

"Ooow." Mandy doubles over and clutches her stomach. "I don't feel good."

"All right, all right," I say, rubbing her back. "Come on. I have an idea. You can go in a pot and I'll go dump it in the potty."

"No!"

"Why not?"

"I don't wann . . . ooo! I'll go outside. I'll use the potty."

"But it's raining, Mandy."

"I don't care. Ooooo!"

"Unh, unh, unh."

"Oh great. Now Casey's up again."

"Ooooo!" cries Mandy, stamping her feet in pain.

"All right, all right!" I put Mandy's jacket and shoes on her, then pick up Casey and wrap him up in a blanket. "Come on," I say, taking Mandy's hand and pulling her out the door.

We run to the pine tree and I push aside the branch, which showers us all with a cascade of icy drops.

"God." I shiver. "We're all going to get pneumonia."

Mandy climbs up on the cold, wet seat, and sits, and sits, and sits.

"Hurry, Mandy, please," I beg.

"Oooh, it hurts," she moans.

"I know. It'll hurt a little. Just go."

"Ooooh ow."

The rain is soaking through my jacket and Casey's blanket is sopping. He begins to fuss and wiggle.

"Come on, Mandy, please!"

"I'm trying!"

"God!" I take my rain-spattered glasses off and shove them in my pocket, then I rub my eyes tiredly with my free hand. How much more can I stand? Look at me, standing here in the night like an idiot while other girls my age are polishing their nails and giggling on the phone.

Tears of self-pity trickle down my cheeks.

"Oww, ow!"

"Dammit, Mandy, just go!" I grab her arm and shake her.

Terror fills her eyes and I jump back and stare at my hand as if it belongs to someone else. Mandy crumples up, grabbing her arm in pain. I hurt her. I deliberately hurt her.

"Oh, Mandy, I'm sorry," I tell her. "I didn't mean to hurt you, I swear."

She stares up at me in pain and bewilderment and I'm so ashamed. I've done it! I've lost control again!

"Please forgive me, Mandy," I whisper, moving in close and stroking her hair. "I'll never hurt you again, I swear."

Never again, Anna. Never again. You'll see. Mama's tearful face comes back to me and I close my eyes against the image.

"I'm not like her," I whisper through clenched teeth. "I'm not."

Mandy lets out one more shuddering cry, and then her pain is over and she has relief. She leans against me in exhaustion.

"Okay, honey, it's all over now," I tell her. "You're going to be okay now."

"I want to go home, Anna," she whimpers weakly.

"I know, baby. I know."

I usher her, pale, wet, and trembling, back to

the cabin and get her and Casey rubbed down. I help them into dry clothes and put them back to bed.

"Anna?" Mandy whimpers again.

"Yes?"

"Can't we go home, please?"

I sigh. "We don't have a home anymore, Mandy."

She puts her thumb in her mouth, rolls over, and starts to hum.

Casey wakes several times in the night, whining and pulling on his ear. By the time morning nears he is screaming. His face is flushed and hot, and his little fists are balled up in pain. I sit with him on my lap, tears of worry streaming down my cheeks. He looks at me in desperation. . . .

It's over, Anna. Give up.

I rise slowly, my heart feeling dead and cold. I carry Casey over to where Mandy is still curled up in her blanket, softly humming.

"Come on, Mandy," I say wearily. "We're going."

She rolls back and looks at me. "Going where?"

"I don't know. Somewhere. We can't stay here."

Mandy sits up, eyes wide. "What will happen to us?" she asks.

"I don't know. But we have to get Casey to a doctor. He's very sick."

Mandy's face is pale with fear, but she asks no more questions. She gets up and dresses quickly.

I take the blue envelope from my backpack, fold it into a tight square and insert it through a little hole in my jacket lining. I look at the silver-handled hairbrush and turn away, leaving it where it lies. I bundle Casey up and grab Mandy's hand and we set off through the rain. The woods are soggy and the brook has overflowed its banks. The trail back to the house will be impassable. We'll have to go through the park. In no time at all we are wet from head to toe. Our feet squish in our shoes and our hair drips in our faces, but we are hurrying so fast that we aren't cold. By the time we reach the lake Casey is frantic. I look down into the water as we cross the bridge, and my heart is filled with loathing.

I hate you, Mama! I want to scream. *I hate you! Look what you've done to us!*

I can't, though, can't let the babies know. Instead I suck all the venom from my heart, suck it up into my mouth, and spit it down into the water, spit it on the yellow glow.

* * *

The lights of Mel's Convenience Store reflect on the wet pavement like a beacon, drawing us in out of the cold, gray dawn. I hesitate before going in and grab Mandy's hand.

"Whatever you do," I whisper, in a last, desperate warning, "don't tell them Mommy's dead."

20

I feel like I'm moving in a dream, being pushed along by events the way people get caught up and pushed along in a crowd. This day has been a blur of strangers, poking us, prodding us, staring into our faces, asking questions that all sound the same. Mel and his wife, the police, the social workers, the doctors and nurses at the hospital, the judge and the lawyer at City Court . . .

Now I sit in a social worker's car with a lap full of papers and brochures, Mandy slumped against my shoulder, and Casey sleeping in the car seat next to me. The social worker, Mrs. Romero, is saying something about the gray house we have just pulled up in front of, but I am so tired I can barely make sense of her words.

"What?" I ask groggily.

"I said, this is where you'll be staying for a while, Anna. Isn't it lovely?"

I look at the neat gray ranch house with its bright yellow forsythia hedge. "Here?"

"Yes." Mrs. Romero looks over the seat and gives me a smile.

"And Mandy and Casey, too?" I ask.

Mrs. Romero laughs. "Yes, I told you that. The McCallums have agreed to take all three of you."

Yes, she has told me that before, but I still can't allow myself to believe it. "Do they . . . Do they know everything?" I ask. "I mean, how much older I am, and that I'm not . . . I mean, that I'm . . ."

"Black? Of course, Anna. We don't spring surprises on our foster parents."

I sink back into the seat. I look at the house again, and the pleasant little neighborhood. "How long will we be here?" I ask.

Mrs. Romero smiles kindly. "Well, hopefully just until you can be reunited with your mother."

Reunited with your mother. I picture the lake, cold and gray, with rain pelting down like icy needles, and I shiver.

Mrs. Romero is staring at me. "Don't you *want* to be reunited with your mother, Anna?" she asks.

A lump rises in my throat and I swallow it down. "Yes . . . of course."

"Because if you don't, we can talk about it." Mrs. Romero looks at me earnestly. "That's why we assigned you a lawyer today. I want you to remember that you have rights, Anna. You don't have to do anything you don't want to do."

I nod. Exhaustion is fogging my mind again. "Okay," I say. "I'll remember."

"Good." Mrs. Romero smiles. "Come on now. Let's go meet your foster parents."

Mandy clings to me like a frightened little monkey, and when Mrs. Romero takes Casey out of his car seat he twists in her arms and reaches for me, too. Mrs. Romero hands him over. "They certainly know who loves them," she says.

I stroke Mandy's hair. "It's okay," I reassure her. "We're all going to be together."

She looks up at me with relief in her eyes, but says nothing.

"The baby seems to be feeling better already," Mrs. Romero chatters as she takes our things from the trunk. "That amoxicillin is great stuff, isn't it?" I nod gratefully.

Mrs. McCallum greets us at the door with an uncertain smile. She is a tall, plain woman with straight, shoulder-length, salt-and-pepper hair. She has a cigarette in her hand, which, in my mind, is one strike against her.

"This is Anna, Roe," says Mrs. Romero, "and Mandy, and little Casey."

Mrs. McCallum nods crisply to me and to Mandy, who is hiding under my arm, then she smiles and coos at Casey, who buries his face in my neck.

"Well, come on in," she says in a gravelly voice, standing aside and motioning us into the house. It is depressingly dark inside and the smell of stale smoke is nauseating. Mrs. McCallum crushes out her cigarette in a nearby ashtray and reaches for Casey. "Here, let me have the baby while you take off your coat," she says.

Casey stiffens at her touch, digs his fingers into my arm and starts to scream. Mrs. McCallum's smile fades. "Hmm," she says, "not very friendly, is he?"

"Oh, he'll come around," says Mrs. Romero. "He's been through so much, Roe, and he's not feeling well either. He has an ear infection, poor thing. Don't let me forget to give you his medicine."

Mrs. McCallum coughs and nods. "Come along then," she says to us. "I'll show you the rooms."

I follow her through the kitchen and living room and down a hall, carrying Casey and dragging Mandy behind me. Mrs. Romero brings up the rear. Mrs. McCallum switches on lights as we go. All the shades and drapes are drawn.

"Can't let the sun in, you know," she says with a nervous laugh. "Fades the upholstery."

The house is like a furniture showroom with perfectly coordinated fabrics and drapes and and delicate little knickknacks everywhere.

Immediately I see trouble ahead for Mandy and Casey.

"Do you have other children, Mrs. McCallum?" I ask.

Mrs. McCallum turns and looks at me. "No," she says, then glances pointedly over my shoulder, at Mrs. Romero. "We had a little girl," she continues, her voice bitter. "Sweetest child that ever lived. Had her for five years. And then they took her back."

Mrs. Romero clears her throat. "Yes, that was sad, Roe," she says. "But those things happen. You knew the mother might return. . . ."

"After five years!" Mrs. McCallum has a fit of coughing. "What kind of mother stays away for five years?" she rasps when she can speak again. "You made a mistake giving that child back, I tell you."

"Yes, well . . . we do the best we can, you know. It's never easy." Mrs. Romero glances uncomfortably at me. "And we do appreciate you opening your heart and home again for these children."

"Yes." Mrs. McCallum nods curtly at Mrs. Romero. "But I won't make the mistake of getting attached again. I can tell you that." She pushes open a door and switches on a light. "This will be your room, Anna," she says.

My room? My trepidations fade as I walk into the room and twirl slowly, trying not to trip over

Mandy, who is hanging onto my jacket. The room is beautiful. Green wallpaper with small pink roses, a thick pink carpet, and a double bed with a ruffled green satin spread and tons of flowered pillows. And white wicker furniture! It is a dream room, something you'd see in a magazine. I am speechless. My room? I have never had a room of my own before. Never.

"And the little ones will be just one door down," says Mrs. McCallum, walking back out into the hall.

I follow reluctantly, not wanting to leave my room. Mrs. McCallum switches on the light in the next room and a delighted little "Oh!" escapes from under my arm. Two wide blue eyes peek out. This was obviously the little girl's room. It is all pink satin, ribbons and lace, and there are dolls everywhere! In one corner a white crib has been set up for Casey.

"Oooh," Mandy croons again.

Mrs. Romero beams. "Didn't I tell you it was a lovely home? I know you're all going to be very happy here." She puts Mandy's and Casey's things down.

"I'll take those," said Mrs. McCallum, picking up the bundles gingerly. "I'm sure I can find them all something to put on until I get these washed."

"They're not dirty," I tell her. "We got them clean from our house this afternoon."

"Yes, well, we'll see," she says, carrying them out of the room at arm's length.

Mrs. Romero turns to me. "I'll be going now," she says. "You have my home and office numbers in your packet. If you need anything, anytime, just call. Meanwhile I'll be stopping by occasionally to see how you're getting along."

I nod.

"And of course we'll be looking into your mother's disappearance, and I'll let you know the minute we find anything."

My heart thumps and I lower my eyes so Mrs. Romero will not see my discomfort. "Thank you," I say quietly.

Mandy creeps out from under my arm and tiptoes over to a big doll that is sitting on a chair in the corner. "Isn't she bea-ootiful, Anna?" she whispers.

I smile as Mandy picks up the doll and hugs it close.

"Please don't touch the dolls!"

Mandy drops the doll, takes one look at the imposing figure of Mrs. McCallum, standing, hands on hips, in the doorway, and darts back under my arm.

"She . . . didn't mean any harm," I tell Mrs. McCallum.

Mrs. McCallum walks over, picks up the doll and places it carefully on the chair again. "These are Amy's dolls," she says. "No one is to touch them. Do you understand?"

I stare at her. "If you say so."

Mrs. McCallum takes a pack of cigarettes from her pocket, slips a cigarette out and taps it on the pack. "All right," she says. "Just make sure nobody touches them. They . . . meant so much to Amy, you know?"

"Whatever you say," I repeat. Casey is getting heavy and I shift him to my other hip.

"All right then. You can . . ." Mrs. McCallum lights her cigarette, sucks in a big drag and gives me a long appraising look. "You can call me Auntie Roe." She blows the smoke slowly out again.

I feel like saying, *Gee, thanks*, and waving her smoke away, but I'm no fool. I know that we're playing with this lady's deck, and she holds all the cards. "That'll be fine," I agree.

Auntie Roe smiles and takes another puff. "Are you always so cooperative?" she asks.

I shrug. "I try to be."

Auntie Roe blows smoke out of her mouth and sucks it back in through her nose again. "This is going to be different," she says. "I've never had a teenager before. I won't put up with backtalk or any of that other adolescent nonsense, you know?"

I nod tiredly.

"All right then, first things first. You all need

a bath. I'll take the baby. You help your sister."

I hold Casey tight. "I don't think he'll go to you yet," I say.

Auntie Roe laughs a short, nervous laugh. "Children don't make the rules in this house," she says. She walks over and pulls Casey from my arms. He stiffens and starts to cry, but she takes no notice. "And you," she says, bending over and peering at Mandy, "come out from under there and stop your foolishness."

21

"I don't like her, Anna."

"Shush!" I put a hand over Mandy's mouth and glance apprehensively toward the bathroom door. "Don't say that."

"Why not? It's true."

"I don't care. We're all together and we've got a roof over our heads. We're even going to be in our same schools. We can't afford to be fussy, Mandy. You be nice to her. I don't care if she's a witch."

Mandy sighs and her little bare shoulders sag. "Why can't we play with the dolls?" she asks.

"I don't know. This lady seems to have some weird hang-up about this Amy kid, but we can live without dolls, Mandy. We can't live without each other, okay?"

Mandy nods slowly and a little tear appears in the corner of her eye. "I miss Mommy," she says.

I pause with a cup of fresh water in my hand. "Do you?" I ask.

Mandy looks up in surprise. "Yes," she says. "Don't you?"

I rest the cup on the side of the tub and stare into the water.

"I don't know," I say. "Tell me what you miss."

"I miss . . . when Mommy used to be happy."

I continue to stare at the water. *When Mama used to be happy?*

"You know . . ." Mandy continues, "when she used to tell us about the boat."

Ah, yes. The boat. Mama's dream. The yacht that she was going to buy someday and sail us in all around the world. I believed in that dream when I was Mandy's age, too.

"Remember?" she asks hopefully.

I smile sadly. "Yes, I remember."

Mandy squeezes the sponge in her hand and listlessly rubs her knees. "I miss when we were all together, too," she says, "in our own house."

A pang of homesickness hits me, and my eyes mist over. "Yes," I say quietly. "I miss that, too."

Mandy looks up at me. "Do you think we'll ever have a home again, Anna?" she asks.

I shake off my sadness and summon up my old resolve. "Yes," I tell Mandy. "We'll have a home again. I don't know how or when, but we will have a home again."

Mandy seems encouraged by my conviction. She smiles and resumes scrubbing herself. I can still hear Casey crying from the kitchen. "Hurry now," I say, pouring clean water over Mandy's head. "Casey's scared and I want you to go out and keep him company while I take my shower."

Mandy wrinkles up her nose. "But I'm scared of that lady, too," she says.

"Don't be," I say as I lift her from the tub. "She's a little odd, but I think she means well. Maybe she'll even get to like us if we're nice. Maybe . . ." I touch the thick, soft towel to my cheek. "Maybe she'll like us so much that she'll want to adopt us, and this can be our home."

Mandy scowls. "Yuck."

I smile and give her little bare bottom a playful swat with the towel. "Never mind yuck. You want to stay together, don't you?"

"Yeah."

"So what's so bad about living here?"

Mandy rolls her eyes. "Auntie Roe."

"Well, maybe *Uncle* whatever-his-name-is will be nicer."

I watch out of the kitchen window as the man gets out of his car. He is a large, pasty-faced, homely man with a slow, listless step. I watch with great curiosity and a little fear. There hasn't been any man in my life for a long time. I'm not sure what it's going to be like living in the same house with one.

"Be quiet now when Elvin comes in," says Auntie Roe. "Elvin doesn't like a lot of commotion."

I shoot a warning look over my shoulder at Mandy, who is setting the table. She nods obediently.

Elvin McCallum opens and closes the front door, jangles the hangers in the front closet, and finally appears in the kitchen doorway, filling it nearly side to side with his girth. I glance at him nervously. His heavy-lidded eyes are dull and expressionless. He has three chins and a bulbous nose, and a fat, damp cigar protrudes from his rubbery lips. He reminds me exactly of the father dinosaur in a sitcom that Mandy used to watch.

"Hello, dear," says Auntie Roe in her raspy voice. "Did you have a good day?"

Elvin grunts and shuffles over to the refrigerator, breathing heavily. I glance at his back as he goes by, half expecting to see a tail.

"These are the new children from DSS," said Auntie Roe. "This is Anna, Mandy, and Casey. Children, this is Uncle Elvin."

"Hello," I say tentatively.

Uncle Elvin eyes me up and down, then turns and does the same to Mandy and Casey. Mandy shrivels under his gaze and sidles over next to me, but Casey is too involved with a cookie to notice. Uncle Elvin says nothing. He opens the refrigerator, takes out a beer, and walks out of the room, leaving behind the mingled fragrances of body odor, cigar smoke, and bad breath.

"You children keep quiet now," says Auntie Roe, "Uncle Elvin and I always watch the news before dinner. Mandy, finish the table please."

Auntie Roe disappears around the corner after Uncle Elvin.

Mandy looks up at me, her nose wrinkled in disgust. "Double yuck!" she whispers.

I laugh silently and put a finger to my lips.

"Three?" I hear a gruff voice in the other room say.

"Shush," Auntie Roe snaps in return. "I told you there were three. You know we need the money."

"For what?" comes the gruff voice again. "More damn knickknacks?"

There is a brief silence, then Auntie Roe speaks in a pouty voice. "I just want to have a nice home," she says. "Is that too much to ask?"

"You didn't say nothin' about the colored one," growls Uncle Elvin.

"They're a package deal," Auntie Roe snaps. "We had to take all or none, besides, I don't see where it's any big deal. She's not *that* dark."

"Yeah, you tell that to the neighbors," Uncle Elvin grunts. Then the TV comes on and the conversation ends.

I glance over at Mandy. She has heard them and there is a dangerous fire in her eyes. She balls her little hand into a fist and starts toward the door. I lunge after her and grab her arm.

"Where are you going?" I whisper.

"I gonna punch that fat man right in the nose," she says.

"You are not!" I whisper, pulling her back away from the doorway.

"Yes, I am," she hisses, "and Auntie Roe, too. I'm not gonna let them say mean things about you."

I can't help but smile. "Listen, Monk," I say, bending down close to her ear. "I don't care what they say. Their words can't hurt me, understand? They can call me Poop if they want, as long as they let us all stay here, together."

Mandy's mouth twists into a grin. "Poop?" she says with a mischievous giggle.

I give her a playful little pinch. "They can call me Poop," I tell her, "not you."

Mandy throws her arms around my neck and squeezes me, but when we pull apart again I can see she is worried. I give her another little squeeze.

"It'll be okay," I assure her, not letting on that I have a pit in my stomach the size of the Grand Canyon. "It'll be okay."

Mandy stares at her dinner plate. "What's that?" she asks.

"What's what?" asks Auntie Roe.

"She means the broccoli," I explain.

Auntie Roe arches an eyebrow. "She's never seen broccoli before?"

I shake my head. "Mama never made us eat vegetables."

Auntie Roe frowns. "Well, in this house you eat what's on your plate."

"But I don't like broculyee," says Mandy.

"I didn't ask you if you liked it," said Auntie Roe. "I told you to eat it."

Mandy glances at me and I nod. She reluctantly pushes a small piece of broccoli onto her fork and puts it into her mouth. Immediately her face begins to contort. She stares at me, eyes pleading.

"You really shouldn't force . . ." I start to say.

"Swallow it," Auntie Roe interrupts.

The expression on Mandy's face is growing more desperate. I glance at Uncle Elvin. He is too busy eating to take any notice of what's going on. He reminds me of a pig, grunting and snorting as he chomps and chews, bits of food clinging to his lips and dribbling down his chin.

"I'm waiting," Auntie Roe warns, staring across the table at Mandy.

Mandy grabs her milk and takes a big gulp, then she nearly gags. Tears appear in the corners of her eyes. "It won't go down," she whimpers.

Uncle Elvin shoves a whole roll into his mouth and washes it down with a huge gulp of beer.

I try once more to reason with Auntie Roe.

"It's really not a good idea to force her." I repeat. "She . . ."

Auntie Roe turns hard eyes in my direction. "Nonsense," she says, then she turns back to Mandy. "Swallow it, now," she demands.

Mandy closes her eyes and swallows. There is a moment of silence, and then Mandy's cheeks bulge, and bulge again, then . . .

"Bl . . .Bl . . . Blaagh!" Out comes the broccoli, and the milk, all over the table.

Uncle Elvin jumps up. "Jee-sus Christ!" he says. Then he tosses his napkin on the table and stomps out of the room.

"Now look what you've done!" Auntie Roe shrieks at Mandy. "You've upset Elvin!"

Mandy and Casey start to cry and Auntie Roe flies out of the room after Uncle Elvin.

I slump back in my chair with a sinking heart. This is never going to work. Never.

22

The kitchen has been cleaned up, and I sit on the edge of the couch, pretending to watch TV while Casey screams in the background. I steal a glance at Auntie Roe, sitting stone-faced in her chair.

"I usually rock him to sleep," I venture hesitantly.

"Obviously," says Auntie Roe. "That's his problem. He's spoiled."

I stare at Auntie Roe, biting my tongue to keep from screaming at her. *Spoiled! He's been abandoned by a woman who used to beat him!* I don't scream, though. I breathe deeply, count to ten, and try again. "I don't mind rocking him," I say pleasantly. "I really enjoy doing it."

"He's old enough to cry himself to sleep," says Auntie Roe. "He'll give up before long."

I look at Uncle Elvin, asleep in his armchair. He looks like he's melting. His jowls flow into his triple chins, which in turn roll down to meet the folds of his chest, ending in the great mound of his belly, which lies like an oversized water balloon in his lap.

I turn back to the TV, trying to keep my mind off Casey's increasingly desperate sobs, but each new wail claws at my heart until my insides feel bloody and raw.

I glance at Roe again. "Maybe if I just went in and talked to him a minute . . ."

"I know what I'm doing," she says. "I've raised plenty of babies. You stay right where you are. If he sees you, it'll only make matters worse."

She dips her hand in a bowl of popcorn, throws a few kernels into her mouth and turns her attention back to the TV. I twist my hands in my lap, remembering Casey's face that day when I came home and found him alone, and the day Mama "accidentally" burned him with her cigarette, and the day . . .

"You don't understand!" I cry, jumping up at last. "He doesn't know what's happening. He's afraid!" I run down the hall and burst through the bedroom door.

"Hey!" shouts Auntie Roe. "You come back here!"

"What the hell is goin' on?!" I hear Uncle Elvin roar.

Mandy bolts up in bed.

"It's okay," I tell her as I rush by. "I've come to help Casey." I pick Casey up and hold him close.

"Shhush now," I murmur, rocking him gently. "Shhush now, baby, Anna's here."

Casey clings to me fearfully, burying his head in my neck. Auntie Roe is standing in the doorway, her eyes smoldering. I stare back, daring her to try and take him from me. She turns and walks away.

"It's okay, baby," I whisper to Casey. "Shush now." I stroke and cuddle him, rocking my body from side to side. He quiets and I begin to hum. He reaches his little hand up to my lips; I kiss his tiny fingers and continue to hum. Gradually he grows soft in my arms and his eyelids droop. When he is soundly asleep I put him back in his crib and tuck his blanket around him. I wink at Mandy and give her hand a little squeeze, then I tiptoe out of the room.

From the kitchen I hear Auntie Roe's cough, and then her voice, talking quietly to Uncle Elvin.

"I'll send her right back," she is saying. "I don't have to put up with this."

My heart begins to thump and I tiptoe closer.

"I say send them all back," says Uncle Elvin. "and just quit spending so much money. Never did know who you're trying to impress."

Auntie Roe huffs. "There's nothing wrong with liking nice things," she says, "besides, I enjoy the children. I really do. Especially when they're good, like Amy. You loved Amy, too. You know you did. I say we give the little ones a chance. It's her that's the problem."

I don't wait for Uncle Elvin's response. I walk into the kitchen, my heart in my throat. "Please," I say, my voice shaking. "I'm sorry. Don't send me away."

Auntie Roe nearly drops her cigarette when I walk in, but she quickly recovers her composure. "Well, you should be sorry, young lady," she says in her gravelly voice. "I've cared for a lot of children in my day, and I don't need you interfering. Two mothers in one house won't work. Do you understand?"

I swallow hard. Mama used to say the same thing. Maybe she was right. Maybe they're both right. Maybe I am the problem. I feel tired, defeated. I don't want to think anymore.

"Yes," I say quietly. "I understand."

"Are you sure?"

"Yes."

"All right. Now go to bed."

Bed. Yes. Bed is what I need. I start across the hall toward my room.

"Uh . . . Not in there," says Auntie Roe.

I turn back, confused. "What?"

Auntie Roe flashes her humorless smile. "I'm sure you'd be more comfortable in with your sister and brother," she says. "Your sister is small. There's plenty of room in the bed."

I stare, still not comprehending. "No, that's

okay," I say. "They're right down the hall. I can hear them if they need me."

Auntie Roe's smile fades. "I'm sure you'd rather sleep in with your sister," she repeats.

I look into her cold eyes, then glance over my shoulder at the beautiful green room. Perfect, like a magazine picture, and apparently meant to stay that way.

"Oh," I say quietly. "All right, that'll be fine." I start to turn away when Auntie Roe touches my arm. Even her fingers are cold.

"We don't have to mention this little change in sleeping arrangements to Mrs. Romero," she says.

"No," I say tiredly. "Good night."

I crawl into bed beside Mandy. The comforter is thick and warm, and the sheets feel deliciously clean and soft after so many nights of sleeping on the hard cabin floor. Mandy wakes slightly, smiles when she sees me, and snuggles next to me. I rest my chin on her head and fall asleep breathing in the soft perfume of her hair.

23

"*Anna,*" *says Mrs.* Andriadi with a cheerful smile. "It's so nice to see you back. We were all so worried about you."

"I'm fine," I say, then I lower my eyes and add, "but I . . . didn't get a chance to finish that report you assigned."

"Oh, don't you worry about that," Mrs. Andriadi tells me. "I'll just figure your average from . . ."

"No," I say quickly, "I don't want any favors, just an extension. I'll have the report done by next week."

Mrs. Andriadi searches my eyes, and then nods. "If that's what you want, Anna," she says, "that will be fine." Then she breaks into a smile again. "I don't think I've ever seen your hair down before," she says. "Very pretty."

I blush and start to back away. "Oh, thanks," I say, "it's kind of wild, but . . ." And then I bump into something, turn, stagger a few steps, trip over a desk and crash to the floor, desk and all.

"Anna!" shrieks Mrs. Andriadi. "Are you okay?"

"Yes," I mumble, red-faced, as I push the desk back up and start to dig myself out of the avalanche of books and papers that have fallen on top of me.

The rest of the class is starting to filter in now and I'm mortified by their stares and giggles. Someone bends to help me and my humiliation is complete.

"I'm fine," I say, pushing my hair out of my face and shoving a geography book off my lap.

"You sure?" Nate's manner is cool, but concerned. He is holding out a hand to help me up.

"Yes, I'm sure," I say, ignoring his hand and struggling to get to my feet on my own.

Nate shakes his head in bewilderment and walks away. My face burns as I hurriedly finish cleaning up the mess I've made, trying to ignore the stares of the class. No one is giggling anymore. They watch me instead in a curious, almost morbid silence. Word is out apparently. Raggedy Anna's mother ran away. Raggedy Anna is in a foster home. Raggedy Anna is even more of a freak than ever. I turn the righted desk over to its waiting owner, stumble back to my own desk and drop into my seat, sliding down as far as I can and burying my face in my history book.

"All right, class," Mrs. Andriadi begins. "Today we will discuss the postwar period. . . ."

I try hard to listen but I can't. I'm completely embarrassed and all too aware of Nate's eyes boring into the back of my head. I dare not turn to face him, not until I can get my emotions under control.

I concentrate on my breathing until my heart slows down and the heat drains from my face. The attention of the class is on Mrs. Andriadi now and I no longer feel the weight of Nate's stare. I can think again. I put my embarrassment aside and think of Nate, of the way I have returned his kindness with cruelty, sabotaging one of the first chances I've had for friendship in a long, long time. Maybe I'm being a fool. Maybe I should take a chance. Life has calmed down a little. For the moment, at least, the babies are safe. Maybe it's okay to think of myself, for a little while anyway. I glance over my shoulder and Nate's eyes meet mine, then he frowns and looks away.

My heart sinks and I turn back to my book. Who am I kidding? I've already blown any chance I had with Nate. And what would be the point, anyway? The secret at the lake is still out there, ticking like a time bomb, waiting at any moment to blow my life apart.

24

I close my math book and look up at the calendar on the McCallum's kitchen wall. May 24. A month. We've been here one month. It seems like years.

Mandy gags over her supper nightly and gets sent to bed without eating more times than not. The sparkle is gone from her eyes and so is the little defiant streak in her personality. She haunts the corners of the house like a small shadow, fearful of irritating Auntie Roe or inciting the wrath of Uncle Elvin.

Casey has learned to cry himself to sleep, but he's also learned not to trust anyone anymore, even me, and he is fretful and unhappy most of the time.

I have learned to keep my mouth shut and do Auntie Roe's bidding without question. I go out of my way to help with the cooking and housecleaning in the hope that she will be content to keep me around. My only pleasures are studying and getting my A's. I keep to myself more than ever. At school Nate doesn't even look at me anymore, and I tell myself it's better this way. But it still hurts.

I'm not beaten, though. I have hope that something will work out for Mandy and Casey and me. There is the tattered blue envelope, tucked away inside my jacket lining waiting for the close of school, just five more weeks away. Then somehow I will find the someone in Mississippi, the someone who might care.

The phone rings and I jump to answer it.

"Hello, Anna?" says the familiar voice of Mrs. Romero. "How are you?"

"Fine," I tell her.

"That's good, dear." I detect an unusual note in Mrs. Romero's voice. "Is Mrs. McCallum at home?" she asks.

"Yes," I say, "just a minute."

Auntie Roe walks in and I hand her the phone. "Did you finish the laundry yet?" she asks me.

"No," I tell her. "I just finished my homework. I'll do it now."

I walk silently down the hall toward the laundry closet, straining to hear the conversation in the kitchen.

"Yes? Oh, hi, Maria," I hear Auntie Roe say, then, in a hushed voice, "What!"

The alarm goes off in my head. I have been fearing this, fearing that as the Memorial Day weekend approached . . .

"Well, I can't say I'm surprised," Auntie Roe is saying. "But what a way to go! You'd think she would've just stuck her head in the oven or something."

My skin feels as cold as ice.

"So what now?" Auntie Roe asks. "Have they found any family yet? No, huh? Me? No, I can't take them long term. I might consider keeping the baby, but not the other two. They've got too many problems. I don't know where you're going to find anyone to put up with them. What? Yes, I know it's sad, but people can only put up with so much, you know?"

I lean against the closet door, feeling suddenly weak.

"No, no," I hear Auntie Roe say. "You can tell them. That's your job. Why don't you come over tomorrow after they get home from school. Okay. We'll see you then."

I stagger down the hall to the bedroom, slip inside and sink into the little chair by the bed. I stare into the darkness, listening to Mandy and Casey's soft breathing. Casey stirs, makes a little sucking noise with his mouth, then falls silent again. I try to swallow down the lump in my throat, but it hurts too much. I close my eyes against the tears, but they well up and spill out anyway. I put my face down into my hands and let them fall.

What now, Anna? I ask myself. *Oh my God! What now?*

25

I lie awake all night, making plans. At dawn I rise and take all of the books out of my book bag. I pack it with some clothes, and tuck in the blue envelope. I walk over to Casey's crib and watch him, memorizing everything: the shape of his face, the way his lashes brush his cheeks in sleep, his button nose, and his little pink mouth.

"I'll be back, Casey," I whisper. "Don't you worry. I'll be back." Then I kiss my fingertips and stroke them feather-light across his cheek.

Mandy stirs and I go over and kneel by her bed.

"Mandy," I whisper. "Mandy, wake up."

She opens sleepy eyes and looks at me. I touch a finger to my lips to warn her to be quiet. Her brow creases and a question forms in her eyes. I search for the right words but there is no easy way to say what must be said. I take her hand in mine.

"I have to go away for a while, Monk," I whisper.

Her eyes widen, and her fingers dig into my hand.

"I won't be gone long," I say hurriedly. "I'm going to look for the person who sent the money." I force a smile and try to sound hopeful. "It might be a daddy, or a grandmother, or someone who will love us."

Mandy shakes her head. "No, Anna," she whispers desperately. "Don't go. Let's just stay here. It's not so bad here."

My smile wilts. "We can't stay here, Monk," I tell her. "They found out about Mommy. The McCallums want to keep Casey, but not you and me."

Mandy stares at me for a long time, then her little eyes flash anger. "They can't have Casey," she says. "He's our baby."

I grin. "You bet he is, and that's why I'm going to go find someone who wants all of us."

Mandy's resolve wavers. "But . . . can't me and Casey come, too?"

I shake my head. "There isn't enough money, Monk. Besides, how far do you think we'd all get before they caught up with us? I can go a lot faster alone."

"But, what am I supposed to do?" asks Mandy.

"You stay right here. I'm telling Mrs. McCallum I'm staying at school late for play try-outs, but when I don't show up this evening, you tell them I probably went somewhere with my new boyfriend."

Mandy's eyes widen. "What boyfriend?"

I smile. "There is no boyfriend, dummy. I just want to throw them off the track. Tell them you don't know his name, but he drives a red car, okay?"

Mandy nods. "But . . . where are you really going, Anna?"

I shake my head once more. "I'm not going to tell you where, because I don't want anyone to follow me and I don't want you to make a mistake and tell them."

Mandy picks at a loose thread in her comforter, pondering all of this, then suddenly she looks up. "Why don't we just tell the social people about the money? Then they can find out who sent it."

I smile. "I wish it was that easy, Mandy, but it's not. That would be too dangerous. Suppose a daddy did send it? You know we don't have the same daddies. What if the daddy who sent it only wants the one of us that's his? What happens to the other two?"

Mandy's hopeful expression fades.

"See," I tell her. "I've got to go check things out. We have to be really careful."

She nods slowly, begrudgingly, then throws her arms around my neck and hugs me tight. "But, I'll miss you, Anna."

"I'll miss you, too, monkey. Every minute. But I'll be back soon. Cross my heart."

I stand at the phone booth outside of the gym, trying to block out the noise behind me.

"What city, please?" asks the operator in a deep southern drawl.

"Sunnydale," I say.

"Yes?"

"Is there . . . Is there a number for an O'Dell?"

"First name please?"

"I don't know it."

There is a short silence and then, "I have two O'Dells, a Roland, and a James."

My heart skips a beat. A James? Casey James. A chill races down my spine and spreads out to my fingers and toes.

"I'd like the number for James, please," I rasp breathlessly.

I jot the number down, and then dial it with shaky fingers. Another operator comes on and tells me to deposit more change, and then the number begins to ring.

Daddy? I cry silently. Daddy, are you there?

A woman answers.

"Oh, hello," I say, trying to keep my voice from trembling. "Is James O'Dell there please?"

"He's not in right now. May Ah take a message?"

"Actually . . ." My voice catches, but I go on. "I'm a friend of his former wife, Suzanne, and I wonder if he might know how I could get in touch with her?"

There is a moment of silence, then the woman asks, skeptically, "A friend of Suzanne's? Why, you sound like a child."

I laugh nervously. "Oh, I know. People tell me that all the time. I wish I looked as young as I sound."

"You don't sound like you're from 'round these parts either," the woman adds.

"No, no I'm not. I'm calling from Connecticut actually. We only lived in Sunnydale a couple of years, but Suzanne and I were such good friends back then, and I was just thinking of her today. . . ."

"Well, you seem to be a bit confused," the woman cuts in. "Suzanne wasn't Jimmy's wife. She was his sister. And she left Sunnydale years ago."

Sister? Then James O'Dell isn't my father. But Mama has a brother. My emotions race up and down.

"O . . . Oh?" I stammer. "Well, maybe I am confused. It was so long ago. Do you know why she left or where she went?"

"No. Ah am sorry. Ah never even met her. She left long before Ah married her brother. My mother-in-law may know more, but Ah don't know if she'll talk to you. Nobody in the family seems to want to say much about Suzanne."

Mother-in-law? That would be my grandmother! My head is spinning so, I can hardly think anymore.

"Oh. Okay. Thank you," I say. "Maybe I will give her a call. What did you say her name was?"

"Mrs. Roland O'Dell."

"Thank you. You've been a great help."

I hang up the phone and sag against the wall. Mrs. Roland O'Dell. My grandmother! I feel giddy. I have found them. I have found my family! Hope bubbles up inside me. But I'm also apprehensive. Why don't they want to talk about my mother? And why did Mama tell me all these years that they were dead?

"Nice shoes, Anna."

I look up. Some girls are standing across the hall, casting sidelong glances at my feet and giggling. I look down at the cheap plastic shoes Mrs. McCallum bought me the other day at a tag sale, and for a moment I don't know whether to laugh or cry. Here I stand at one of the most critical junctures of my life, and these girls have nothing better to do than make fun of my shoes! It is all too much suddenly, and I feel tears slipping down my cheeks.

At the sight of my tears, the girls stop giggling and walk away.

"God," I hear one of them say, "what a baby!"

* * *

I wait for Nate after last period history class. I hate turning to him again under the circumstances, but I have no one else.

He slips by in the crowd that pours through the door and I hurry after him, calling out his name. He turns and regards me unsurely.

"Yeah?"

"Can I talk to you a minute?"

He says nothing but pauses long enough for me to catch up.

I wait for the crowd in the hall to thin before speaking. "I need your help," I say quietly.

Nate frowns. "My help? Why?"

"It's about my mother," I hurry to explain, "and I wouldn't ask if it wasn't really important. Can you meet me at the cabin this afternoon?"

The old compassion flickers in Nate's eyes for a moment, but then he turns cool again. "I would," he tells me, "but I can't. I've got baseball practice."

"This evening then?"

Nate hesitates. "I don't get it," he says. "I thought you didn't want me around."

I'm growing nervous and impatient. "Look," I say, pleading with my eyes, "I'm desperate, okay? Can you help me or not?"

Nate looks at me for a long minute, then nods. "All right. I'll be there."

I sigh with relief. "Thanks. And can you bring some stuff?"

"What kind of stuff?"

"A pair of scissors, a baseball cap, and some real boyish-looking clothes."

Nate arches an eyebrow. "What for?"

"I'll explain when you get there. Just can you? Please?"

Nate studies my face a moment longer. "All right," he says. "I'll see what I can find."

26

I *sit on* the steps of the old porch, waiting and thinking and watching. The mountains all around wear fuzzy coats of new spring-green now, and the trees are so bright that the woods almost glow. Curly little fern fronds and wild lilies-of-the-valley poke up through the old brown leaves on the forest floor, mingling their sweet scents with the musky smell of sun-warmed earth. A chorus of birdsongs echoes in the trees, and across the brook a pair of mourning doves call to each other in soft, sad voices. I bend over and trace a pattern in the dirt with a stick. My heart is heavy, as sad as the mourning dove's song. I wish I could stay, wish that somehow this old cabin could have worked out. I think I could be content here forever, shut away from the world and all its pain.

I snap my stick in half and throw it on the ground. Then I look up at the early evening sky. "Why do you hate me?" I cry. "*Why?* What have I ever done to you?"

A movement catches my eye and my head swivels. Nate stands below the hill, by the brook. My cheeks grow warm. Why does he always arrive at the worst moments? If he has heard me, though, he gives no sign. He jumps the brook and climbs the hill.

"Hi," he says stiffly when he reaches the porch. "I brought the stuff you wanted." He lowers his backpack to the ground.

"Thanks," I tell him. We both look at each other, blush and look away.

Nate shuffles his feet in the dirt. "So," he says after a while. "What's this all about?"

A lump rises in my throat. I don't feel like telling him. Not like this. Not with all these bad feelings between us. The silences stretches on.

At last Nate snorts and throws his hands up in the air. "You are the most frustrating person I've ever met," he says. "Are you going to talk or should I just leave?"

I look up at him but the lump in my throat is getting bigger and I can't seem to force any words out around it.

"All right, fine," he says, dropping his hands to his sides. "I'll go. Is that what you want?" He turns and starts to walk away.

"No," I say, finding my voice at last. "Don't go."

"Well, what then?" Nate asks. "Why won't you tell me what's going on?"

"It's just . . ." I shrug helplessly. "I guess I'm afraid to trust you."

"Trust me?" Nate shakes his head in bewilderment. "What are you talking about? What's going on with your mom?"

I stare at the ground, my eyes fixed on the empty space in front of me, the space where there are no feelings. "She's dead," I hear a distant voice say. "She killed herself."

There is a gasp and I turn and Nate's ashen face comes into focus.

"God," he whispers. "That's awful."

I nod. "Yeah."

Nate's face fades and I'm staring at the space again, the space between him and me, but Nate reaches through and takes my hand.

"I'm *really* sorry, Anna," he says.

The mist clears away and I'm looking into his eyes. They are tender, caring, compassionate. He leans forward and kisses me gently, then he touches his cheek to mine and whispers again, "I'm sorry."

Tears well up in my eyes and I lay my head on his shoulder and cry.

Nate shakes his head. "Please don't make me cut your hair," he says. "I love your hair."

"It'll grow back," I insist. "I've got to look like a boy. As soon as they figure out I'm missing they'll be checking the bus and train stations for a girl."

Nate frowns. "Can't you just tuck it up inside the hat?"

"It's too thick," I say. "Look." I pull Nate's hat on over my topknot and it sits up in the air like a chicken on an ostrich egg. I yank the hat off again, and take my glasses off, too, then I sit on the step in front of Nate. "Here," I say, handing him the scissors. "Cut."

But he doesn't cut. "Don't make me, Anna," he says. "I don't like this—any of it."

"I don't like it either," I admit. "But I'm out of choices. This family is my only hope. Even if they don't want us, maybe they know who my father is, or where my father is. And if he's not around, maybe he's got some family or something. I've got to go check it out."

"So why not just call these O'Dells and ask them to come up here?" Nate asks.

I shake my head. "I can't take that chance. I have to check them out first, make sure they're okay."

"And what if they're not? What if they're a bunch of weirdos?"

My shoulders sag. "I don't know. I guess I'll cross that bridge when I come to it."

"Why can't you just stay with the McCallums?" Nate asks. "Maybe they'll adopt you."

I frown. "They told DSS they'd keep Casey, but not Mandy and me."

Nate grunts. "That stinks."

I grunt my agreement.

"Who wouldn't want you and Mandy?" he says. "I'm sure somebody will."

"That's not the point, Nate," I tell him. "The point is, I don't want us to be split up, you know?"

"Yeah, I know." Nate sighs. "I still think you're crazy, though, taking a bus to Mississippi and dropping in on these people you've never met in your life. Don't you think you should at least talk to them first?"

"I can't. Not until I get some answers."

"What kind of answers?"

"Like, why did Mama run away from them? Why did she say all these years we had no family? Why would they send money, but never call, or write?"

"And how do you plan to find all that out?"

"I don't know. Poke around town, I guess. Ask questions."

"And suppose the money didn't even come from them? Suppose your mother was blackmailing somebody. Did you ever think of that?"

"Yeah. I thought of that. I've thought of everything there is to think of." I tilt my head back and look up into Nate's eyes. "But it's still my only hope, and I'm going for it."

Nate shakes his head in exasperation, but

then a grudging smile tugs at his lips. "You're a tough lady," he says.

I smile. "Yes, I know. Now, cut my hair."

"How does it look?" I ask, when Nate is done.

He scrutinizes my face critically. "I can't tell," he says. "It's kind of sticking out all over. Hey, wait a minute. I think I saw a hairbrush inside."

Before I can stop him, he jumps up and dashes into the cabin. I look down at the long curlicues of hair that lie at a heap around my feet. A minute later Nate comes out with Mama's silver-handled brush. I stare at it as he approaches and touch the uneven stubble on my head.

"No," I say quietly as Nate lifts the brush to my head. "Don't use that."

"Why not?" asks Nate, examining the brush. "It's not dirty or anything."

"Just don't," I say.

Nate looks into my eyes, then lays the brush aside. "Okay," he says combing through my shorn locks with his fingers. His hands move quickly at first, smoothing, shaping, then they slow, stroking, caressing. They cradle my face and I close my eyes and tilt my head up and we kiss.

"You're beautiful, Anna," Nate whispers.

Beautiful.

I look into his eyes, still fearing to believe that it's true.

"Don't be silly," I stammer, reaching up to touch my shaggy hair. "Look at me."

Nate smiles and playfully plunks his hat on my head again. "In case you haven't noticed," he says, "I have been looking at you, for a long time."

I blush happily and adjust the hat on my head. "Will I pass for a boy?" I ask.

"Hmm . . . let's see." Nate darts in under the brim of the cap and kisses me again. "Nope," he says, "lips are way too sweet."

I laugh and push him away. "You'd better go," I say. "It's getting dark."

Nate sighs. "Yeah, I know. I'll leave you my bike. It's down in the woods near the entrance."

"You don't have to do that. I can walk."

Nate shakes his head. "It's fifteen miles to the city from here," he says. "I don't want you walking all that way alone."

I smile. It feels good to have someone watching out for me, caring what I do.

"Just chain it to the bike stand in the park," he goes on. "I'll go in and pick it up tomorrow." He takes a last look around the cabin. "Are you sure you're going to be okay here tonight?"

I nod. "I've slept here before. I can take care of myself."

Nate shakes his head. "I *really* don't like this."

"I'll be fine," I insist.

Nate pulls me into his arms and holds me

tight. "Why does it seem like you're always running away?" he whispers into my hair.

Goose bumps break out on my skin and I pull back. "Don't say that," I tell him. "Don't you ever say that again."

27

I sit on the bus, trying not to think about the fact that I have spent nearly every penny I had on a one-way ticket to Mississippi. I'm only dimly aware of the scenery that whizzes by my window hour after hour. Forty-five hours all told, the ticket agent told me. Forty-five hours from Westbridge, Connecticut, to Sunnydale, Mississippi. So far away from Mandy and Casey. If my mind weren't in such chaos this would be a great adventure, but as it is I can hardly keep track of where I am.

The bus tires hum monotonously. I lay my head back and try to sleep but I can't. The worry wolves are darting in and out of my thoughts. What if these people want nothing to do with me? How will I get back without money? Or worse, what if they do want me, but not Mandy or Casey, and they don't let me go back? Or even more likely, what if they want Mandy and Casey, and not me?

Mama, how could you leave us like this!

Mama. I open my eyes and stare out the window. They're probably burying her today. . . . Where? I wonder. Who will be there to say goodbye? My jaw muscles tighten and I narrow my eyes. I don't care. I feel no pity. She didn't say good-bye to us either.

I close my eyes once more and try to summon thoughts of Nate and hold them up like a torch to keep the wolves at bay. I smile to myself, remembering the warmth of his kiss, the tenderness of his touch.

"You are beautiful, Anna," he said. *Beautiful.*

I am beautiful, Mama. Why didn't you want me to know?

It is noon of the second day when we reach St. Louis, and I catch my first glimpse of the Mississippi. Mama's river. It isn't muddy and brown as I had expected, but wide and blue. Towboats push barges up and down its length and a paddle steamer chugs along like a scene from a picture postcard. The spirit of the river catches me immediately, and I remember the fondness in Mama's voice when she spoke of it. Why did she leave it? I wonder. If it were my river, it would have called to me, the way my mountains are calling me now. Telling me to hurry back where I belong. Calling me home.

It is still dark when we pull into Vicksburg at

five A.M., and I am dull with the lack of sleep. I wash up in the terminal lounge, buy myself a Coke and a package of peanut butter crackers, and stretch out on a bench, using my backpack for a pillow. I doze fitfully, keeping one eye on the clock. The first bus for Sunnydale will leave at 7:15.

Nothing seems real. I feel as if I'm watching a movie in which I'm the main character, and I think vaguely that perhaps I will write all of this down in a book someday. But only if it has a happy ending. I could not live it again otherwise.

A policeman strolls by and pauses near my feet. I tense and resist the urge to pull my baseball cap lower over my face. That would only arouse suspicion. Instead I smile and say, "Morning." He smiles, too, then nods and moves on. I congratulate myself on both making the right choice, and being a good actress. Perhaps I will make my book into a movie, and star in it, too.

At last my bus arrives and I'm on my way. I'm wide awake now and feel a growing excitement inside of me. This is Mama's world, the streets and pathways of her childhood. Here, perhaps, I will find the missing pieces to the puzzle that was Mama.

Vicksburg is a plain little city, sitting on a bluff overlooking the river. It is nothing like I expected, which was, I guess, *Gone With the*

Wind. I mention my disappointment to the lady in the seat next to me and she laughs.

"That would be Natchez," she tells me, "just a little farther south. You go on down there if you want to see the Old South."

I smile and thank her, thinking with a little shiver of excitement that maybe I will one day, with my grandparents, or . . . or maybe even my father.

Rolling north out of the city we pass a cemetery where thousands of tiny white headstones stretch away like rows of teeth, as far as the eye can see. Soldiers, killed in the Battle of Vicksburg, my seatmate tells me. Something stirs in me as I realize that some of them might be related to me. There are roots here, roots old and deep. Why did Mama choose to cut them and drift away?

The land flattens and stretches out to meet the river. Slow-moving tributaries curve in toward the highway and veer off again, and cows graze on the lush, green pastures that lie in between. And then we reach the cotton fields, broad and wide and dusty, with clusters of impoverished little shacks here and there, not much different, I imagine, from the ones that were here in sharecropping days. Another shiver runs down my spine as I realize that this is my history, too. Parts of me are waking up inside, parts I never knew existed. My anger toward

Mama deepens. What gave her the right to take my past away?

At last the bus rolls into a pretty little town with a tree-shaded main street.

"Sunnydale," the bus driver announces, and I crane my neck to look out the window. Flowers are in bloom everywhere, and long, fuzzy horsetails of Spanish moss sway in the breeze, dripping from the branches of vine-covered trees. And of course there are the magnolias. I remember Mama speaking of these. She never spoke of the people or the places, but of the flowers and the trees . . . and the river.

A couple of other people follow me down the aisle out the door, and soon the bus roars away. The others hurry off in different directions and I envy them. They have places to go.

I slowly survey the town. It's a folksy kind of place, with a couple of churches, a few stores, a white columned town hall, and an old-fashioned gas station with a house attached to it. There is a green with a wrought-iron fence, and in its center stands a small gazebo ringed by flower gardens. Black and white people in nearly even numbers cross the green and stroll the streets. Most seem unhurried. They smile and wave to each other. On benches under the moss-covered trees, old folks sit with their morning coffee and chat. So this is Mama's town. The place where she was born. *Mama's town.*

I cross the street and walk through the green to the gazebo. Two little kids chase each other in and out of it. Did Mama play here, too? I wonder. Did she stroll down Main Street to church on Sundays? Walk hand in hand through these gardens with her boyfriends—maybe even with my father?

I look around me at the people on the streets. Most still seem to congregate with others of their own race. Could Mama walk hand in hand with my father in a town like this back then?

My mind fills with questions and I'm anxious to begin finding answers. I cross the street again to the gas station, squeeze into a phone booth, and leaf through the thin yellow book. I find the O's and run my finger down the page.

Roland O'Dell. It's here. It really is here. My grand-father's name. My grandfather's address. *201 Maiden Lane.*

28

I stand staring at the squat little white house across the street, my heart pounding, my hands sweating. My grandparents live there. My mother grew up there. These are my roots, my beginnings. I want to run right up, pound on the door and announce who I am, but the wiser part of me holds back. Something happened in this family. Something went wrong. I want to blame Mama, want to believe that she was the trouble and that these people are decent and good, but a voice inside my head warns me not to jump to conclusions.

I don't see anyone moving in or near the house, but I'll wait, and watch. A young mother comes up the street pushing a stroller, and I do not wish to be seen. I climb inside an ancient rhododendron bush on the corner, being careful not to anger the bees buzzing busily among the blossoms. I settle into one of the crotches and put my backpack on the ground. The dirt is hard packed and the surface roots of the old bush are gnarled and shiny. Children have played here for many years. Maybe even Mama. I shiver again. It feels strange, glimpsing her past this way— sad, like finding some lost puzzle pieces long after the puzzle has been thrown away.

It's a warm day, but I am comfortably cool inside the rhododendron. I doze on and off as the morning passes, waiting for a sign of movement. By the time the sun is high in the sky I have committed every inch of the house to memory. It's not a wealthy-looking home, but it is neat and nice—white clapboard with a flatish black roof and a porch all across the front. There is a swing on one end of the porch and two comfortable-looking rockers under a window. A magnolia tree hangs over the porch, scenting the air with its waxy white blossoms. I picture a little blond girl sitting on the swing pumping her feet back and forth, rocking the swing and making her long hair fly in the breeze. She is smiling and I can't help but smile, too, thinking of her. She looks like Mandy. Suddenly I'm homesick, missing Mandy and Casey, wishing they could be here, sharing this with me. This is our history.

At last a car comes down the street and slows in front of the house. I watch it turn into the driveway and stare as the passenger door opens and a woman gets out. She straightens up and turns toward me and for a moment my heart nearly stops. It's like seeing a ghost! A little thinner per-haps, and a little older, but the face is the same. *Mama!*

My heart starts beating again, jerky and irreg-ular at first, then racing out of control.

The woman takes a key from her purse and lets herself in the side door of the house, and I stand up. I start walking. And then I'm running. I can't let her go like this, can't let her out of my sight. I have found her at last and I can't lose her, not even for a moment. I bang on the front door, not knowing what I'm going to do or say, only knowing that I can't let her get away. The door opens and now the woman is standing in front of me.

"Yes?" she says.

All I can do is stare, just stare at the familiar contours of the face. Adrenaline is pumping through my body but my feet are rooted to the ground, my eyes riveted on the eyes of the woman before me.

"What is it, boy?" the woman asks, a hint of irritation in her voice.

"I . . . uh . . ." My voice cracks and I can't go on.

"Yes?" The woman's brows knit together.

"Do . . . do you have a daughter named Suzanne?" I blurt out.

The woman's expression darkens. "What business is that of yours?" she asks.

I reach up and pull off my hat. "I'm her daughter," I say.

The woman's face blanches. Then, quickly, she recovers.

"Ah'm sorry," she says. "You must be mistaken."

She starts to push the door shut, but frantically I push it back.

"No," I say. "No, I'm not! Suzanne O'Dell is my mother. And she's your daughter. I know. Your daughter-in-law told me so."

The woman presses her lips into a tight line, glancing nervously up and down the street.

"All right, you can come in," she says, pulling the door open again, "but only for a minute."

29

I follow the woman through a dark, shady living room and into a bright kitchen. A fan drones in the window and sunny yellow curtains dance in the breeze it makes. My adrenaline rush is gone and I'm getting a bad feeling inside. This isn't the greeting I was hoping for.

The woman's purse is on the counter. She reaches for it and pulls out a wallet. "How much does she want this time?" she asks.

I am confused. "What?"

"How much does she want?" the woman repeats. "She put you up to this, didn't she? Here. You tell her this is all Ah can afford." She pushes a wad of bills at me.

My stomach turns over. "I didn't come here for money," I say.

The woman gives me a puzzled frown. "What then?"

"I . . ." My throat feels tight but I force myself to go on. "I just wanted to meet you. I thought you might . . . care about me."

The woman stares.

"Care about you?" She repeats my words slowly, with incredulity in her voice, as if this is the oddest idea she has ever heard.

I can feel a deep flush creeping up my neck toward my face. "Never mind," I say, backing away. "This is a mistake. I'll be going now." I turn to flee, but in my haste I trip over a chair and sprawl across the floor.

"Good heavens!" the woman cries. She hurries over to help me up but I scramble away, refusing her hand.

"Are you all right?" she asks.

"Fine," I say, getting to my feet and heading for the door again.

"Wait." The woman's voice is a little less harsh now. "Where is your mother?" she asks. "And why are you dressed like that, like a boy?"

"It doesn't matter," I say. "I have to go."

"Wait, Ah say!" the woman insists. "You wait now or Ah'll call my husband."

Fear gnaws at my belly and I turn and look back at her. "Your husband?"

"Yes. He's the Chief of Police 'round here, you know, or didn't your mother tell you that?"

"My mother never told me anything," I say. "That's why I came. I wanted to know."

"You mean, you ran away?"

"Sort of."

"And your mother doesn't know you're here?"

"No. She doesn't know."

The woman picks up her purse again and stuffs the bills back in. She stares at me a long moment and slowly shakes her head. "You shouldn't have come," she says. "There's nothing for you here."

"I can see that," I say quietly. "I'll be going now."

"Well." The woman sighs. "Have something to eat at least, before you go, and tell me . . ." She looks toward the door and her voice drops, "how your mother is."

"I'm not hungry," I say.

The woman looks back at me and her expression changes suddenly, as if she has put a mask on. "Oh, nonsense. Of course you are," she says. She grabs my hand and pulls me to the table. "Sit down here now and have a glass of lemonade at least."

I sink reluctantly into the chair she has pulled out for me and she pours us both a drink.

"Here," she says, handing me a glass and sitting down across the table.

I take the glass and set it down without drinking.

The woman takes a long gulp, eyeing me over her glass. "You have her features," she announces when she is through. "How is she?"

"Fine."

"What has she done with her life?"

"Don't you know?"

"How would Ah know? Ah don't hear a word from her unless she needs money, and then that's all she says. Never a question about the family or anything. It's obvious she don't care about us, so why should we care about her?"

I look down and fidget with the glass in my hands.

"Did she ever . . . marry?" the woman asks.

I shake my head.

"Any other children?"

My throat feels tight again. "No."

"Just what *has* she told you about us?" the woman asks.

I look up. "Nothing."

"Oh, *Ah'll* bet." The woman laughs strangely and takes another drink of her lemonade. "Ah'll bet she told you a pack a lies."

"She never told me anything," I repeat.

"Well, *Ah'll* tell you." the woman says. "Ah'll tell you because Ah want you to know the truth. The truth is, your mother is a tramp!"

The woman says this with such venom that I wince.

"That's right," the woman goes on tilting her glass from side to side, "a cheap little tramp. Why, she wasn't any older than you when she started running with this one and that one, stayin' out all night. Don't know how she got like that. She surely wasn't raised that way. Just had the devil in her, I guess."

She grips the glass and grimaces. "Why, she even had the nerve," she says in a low, spiteful voice, "to come to me with lies about her father and her brother."

A bitter taste rises in my mouth.

"Sick, filthy lies . . ." the woman goes on. She takes another gulp of lemonade and shudders at the memory.

"How . . . how did you know they were lies?" I ask.

The woman looks away out the window again and for a moment I catch of glimpse of something behind her mask. Is it pain? But the moment passes and she turns back again.

"Of course they were lies!" she snaps. "Ah guess Ah know my own husband, don't Ah? And my Jimmy? She was just born bad, that girl. A bad seed is all."

I'm seeing the little girl on the swing now and my heart is aching for her, for her lost innocence, her lost smile. . . .

"We tried," the woman goes on. "Lord knows we tried. We didn't turn our backs on her, and Lord knows no one in their right mind woulda blamed us if we had."

My stomach hurts and my head is starting to pound. I want to escape, just get away and forget I've ever come. All I want is to go home.

Home to Mandy and Casey. Home to my family.

"Why, we even put up with her pregnancy, all of us walkin' around, our heads hung down in shame. We put up with it though, until the baby came and we saw what it was. The humiliation! She did it just to spite us. We know she did."

I'm staring at this woman now, and my mouth hangs open in astonishment. What "it" was? "It?" *I'm "it!"* I want to scream. It would be useless though. I can see that. I stand up.

"I've got to go," I say. "I've got a bus to catch."

"Oh." The woman stands up, too. "Yes, well . . . that's good. Ah mean, like Ah said, there's nothing for you here."

I nod and turn away.

"Wait." The woman walks over and grabs her purse again. "Here," she says, pressing a wad of bills into my hand.

I stare at the money. "Why?" I ask.

"Why what?"

"Why do you give her money if you hate her so much?"

The woman flushes and I glimpse something behind her mask again. "Well," she blusters. "She's my daughter after all. Can't just turn my back on her, can Ah?"

I loathe this woman and pity her, too. She is weak, worse than Mama. She did turn her back on her own daughter. For what? Security? To save face in the community? I want to throw the money at her. Tell her to keep it, *and* her guilty conscience, but I'm no fool. I've just been handed my ticket back home. I don't say thanks, though. Won't give her the satisfaction. I stuff the bills in my pocket, pull my hat back on and turn away.

I stop at the door, remembering what this nightmare encounter has nearly made me forget.

"About . . . my father?" I say.

The woman nods. "Yes. James Hughes. What about him?"

"Do you know where he is?"

The woman sighs. "You mean she never told you that either?"

"Told me what?"

"He's dead, dear. Killed himself, not long after you were born."

My shoulders sag with the weight of this news. "No," I say quietly. "No, she never told me."

30

I scuff along in the dirt at the side of the road feeling drained and defeated. I don't know where I will turn now, what I will do. But I do know one thing. I will never, ever, let Mandy or Casey fall into the hands of that woman. Somehow I will find another answer.

My mind grows fuzzy and my body is bone tired. My mountains are calling me, cool and green and soft. Home, they are calling. Come home. I find myself back at the gas station and get myself a Coke out of a rusted old machine. I take a gulp and then poke my head into one of the bays. A black man in greasy overalls is busy under the hood of a car.

"Excuse me," I say. "Can you tell me when the next bus to Vicksburg is due?"

The man looks up. "That won't be till mornin'," he says.

"Morning?" My heart sinks. I want to go now. Back to my mountains, my babies, and Nate.

"You're not from 'round these parts," says the man.

"No." I shake my head. "Just visiting."

"Oh? Visitin' who?"

I grope through my foggy mind for a name. "James . . . James Hughes."

The man raises an eyebrow. "Do tell? Have a nice visit, did you?"

Suddenly the mist in my mind clears and I realize I've just made a mistake, maybe a big one. In my exhaustion I have let my guard down. This is a small town. Chances are everybody knows everybody else. I am poised, ready to run. "Yeah," I say. "Very nice."

The man straightens up and closes the car hood. He pulls a greasy rag from his back pocket and walks across the bay, wiping his hands.

I take another sip of Coke and try to act relaxed and unconcerned.

"Now that's interestin'," the man says, peering down at me, "'cause James Hughes has been dead for nearly fifteen years."

I swallow, and the gulp of Coke feels like a charcoal briquette sliding down my throat.

"You a runaway, son?" the man asks.

I shake my head, but before I can move the man grabs my wrist.

"Well, why don't we give the police a call and make sure," he says.

The police! I start to panic. That woman said her husband was the Chief of Police!

"No, please," I beg. "Don't call the police. I'll tell you who I am. I'll tell you everything."

I sit in the neat little kitchen of the gas-station owner's house with my hat on the table in front of me. The owner, Jacob Stevens, and his wife, Birdie, sit across from me. I am weary but concentrating hard, choosing my words carefully, trying to say enough, but not too much.

"So you see," I say finally. "I'm not running away. Not really. I'm heading back as soon as I can get a bus. I just had to come down here and find the answers to all the questions Mama won't talk about."

Jacob pulls at his chin and shakes his head in wonderment.

"Jamie's little girl," he says. "Don't that beat all." He looks me over carefully. "Yeah." He nods. "Ah can see it now. You look like her—your mama—'cept darker of course." He chuckles.

Outside, a car horn honks and Jacob looks up.

"Ah'll mind the station," Birdie says, getting to her feet. She rests a hand on my shoulder and looks into my eyes. "Jacob was your daddy's friend," she says. "He'll tell you what you need to know."

Jacob nods and Birdie pats his hand on her way out the door.

Jacob gets up and walks over to the counter. He pulls a loaf of bread out of a bread box. "Tuna, or bologna?" he asks.

I shake my head. "I'm not hungry."

"Well, Ah am," says Jacob, "and Ah hate to eat alone." He piles two slices of bread with bologna. "Mustard?"

"Um . . . yes, please."

He slides a sandwich under my nose and pours a glass of milk. "Eat," he says. "Ah'll be right back."

I bite into the sandwich, surprised at how good it tastes. I am hungrier than I thought.

"Here it is," says Jacob, walking back into the room with a book under his arm. He sits down beside me and opens the book. He leafs through a few pages, then presses the book out flat in front of me.

"There he is," he says.

I lean forward. It's an old high school yearbook, and on the pages are rows of black and white faces. I look at the picture Jacob points to. "James Hughes," it says underneath.

My chest fills and my eyes grow moist. I blink to clear them and touch a trembling finger to the page. The face is darkly handsome and my own eyes look back at me, bright, inquisitive, thoughtful.

Daddy.

I pick up the book and hug it, and the tears spill down my cheeks. "Tell me about him," I say.

Jacob smiles, but tears shine in his eyes, too. "He was a good man," he says. "A good man, and a good friend. Smart, too, and handsome, but you can see that. He wanted to be a teacher." Jacob gently pulls the book from my arms and turns it to another page. "Future Teachers of America," he says, pointing at James Hughes again, in a group picture this time.

I look at the picture, then read the caption under it. "History is a race between education and catastrophe."

Jacob nods. "Mmm," he says, "H. G. Wells said that, and ain't it the truth?" He shakes his head sadly.

I look back down at my father's face, brimming with hope, bright with ambition.

"What happened?" I ask.

Jacob leans in and looks at James Hughes, too. "Ah guess catastrophe caught up with him first," he says softly.

"What kind of catastrophe?" I ask.

Jacob flips through the yearbook again until he comes to a picture of a pretty young girl with shining blond hair. "That kind," he says.

I don't have to read the name below the picture. "Mama?" I say quietly.

Jacob nods.

"Did she love him?" I ask.

Jacob looks at me thoughtfully. "I didn't know at first," he says. "It was all pretty scandalous back then—a white girl and a black boy . . ." He shakes his head and clucks his tongue. "Didn't happen in Sunnydale. No sirree. Especially not when the girl was the police chief's daughter. Lots of folks thought she was just using James to get back at her daddy and at that big old brother of hers." Jacob hesitates and looks at me as if weighing how much he should say.

"I heard something about that," I tell him. "Was it true?"

"You mean about her daddy and her brother?"

"Yeah."

Jacob nods sadly. "'Fraid so. From what she told James, Ah guess they used her pretty bad."

I look away, my stomach balled up in pain at the ugliness of it all.

"So, it's true then," I say bitterly. "I was Mama's revenge. A little black bastard to throw in her family's face."

Jacob reaches over and touches my hand. "No, darlin'," he says. "Forgive me if Ah led you down that track. That . . . there may have been a grain of truth in it in the beginning. Ah don't know. But Ah can tell you this. When you were born, she loved you. She loved you fierce. And James did, too. And when she came to live with James Ah think she loved him, too. I don't see how she couldn't. He was a hard man not to love."

I look into Jacob's kind eyes, wanting to believe what he believes.

"Then why did my father kill himself?" I ask Jacob.

His eyes harden. "Who told you that?" he asks.

"My . . . Mrs. O'Dell," I say. I will never call that woman grandmother again.

Jacob frowns. "That's what she'd like to believe," he says, "but Ah'll never believe it. James loved livin'. And he loved your Mama, and more than anything in the world, he loved you."

I'm staring at Jacob. "So what are you saying?" I ask.

"Well, Ah can't prove it," he says. "Ah sure wish Ah could. But Ah believe what your Mama believes."

"What Mama believes?"

Jacob nods. "Ah believe that it was a police car that forced Jamie's old Ford off the bridge that night. And not just any police car either. The one that just happened to be scheduled for a new paint job the next day. Chief O'Dell's."

I sit staring at Jacob, my mind reeling. This is too much, all of it. Too much to take in.

"But that's murder," I say.

"Yes." Jacob nods again. "That's why your mama left. She packed you up a few days later and headed north. Said she never wanted you to know this town existed."

I slump back in my chair, weak with emotion, but then out of the swirling eddies in my mind a thought surfaces.

"What was that you said again?" I ask Jacob. "About the way my father died?"

"He drowned," says Jacob. "His car went off a bridge."

I stare at Jacob for a long time, prickles racing up and down my spine, then I pick up the yearbook, fold it closed and hug it tight. *She loved him.*

Jacob squeezes my arm gently. "You keep that book now," he says. "Old thing was just collectin' dust around here anyway."

31

It's Thursday morning by the time I reach Connecticut again, a humid, hazy day. I haven't slept or eaten much in the time I've been away, except for the night I spent with Birdie and Jacob. It's been almost a week since I've seen Mandy and Casey and I have to fight the urge to run to them. I have to move cautiously if I want to be able to sneak them out of the McCallum house, and I'm going to need help.

It takes me nearly the whole day to walk the fifteen miles from the bus station to Nate's house, darting for cover, keeping out of sight. The worry wolves nip at my heels every step of the way. What if Nate won't help me? What if we get caught? What if the McCallums have already sent Mandy away? I reach Nate's house and hide in the woods waiting for him to get home from baseball practice. Everything is going to be okay, I tell myself. Everything is going to be okay.

Around five o'clock Nate's mother's Jeep Cherokee pulls into the driveway. Nate climbs out and his younger sister darts out of the house with her gymnastics bag and jumps in in his place. I see a couple of other little heads in the backseat.

"Turn the oven on three-fifty," I hear Nate's mother yell to him as she backs out again. "We'll be back in an hour."

"Pssst!" I whisper as Nate starts toward the house.

When he turns aroud and sees me, his face lights up. He takes a step in my direction.

"No," I whisper. "Stay there. Don't let on that I'm here."

Nate shakes his head and keeps coming. "Don't worry," he says. "They're all gone now. No one's home but me."

I stand then and run to give him a hug.

"Are you okay?" he asks.

"Yes, just tired."

He squeezes me tight and gives me a welcoming kiss. "How did it go?" he asks.

"I found them," I say.

"You did?" Nate's eyes widen. "What happened?"

I sigh. "It's a long story."

"Come on in then," says Nate, taking my hand. "I'll fix you something to eat and we can talk."

"Are you sure it's safe?"

"Yes, I'm sure. They won't be back for an hour."

* * *

Nate stares at the open yearbook on his lap and shakes his head in disbelief.

"Murder?" he said. "Are you sure?"

"Well, nobody could prove it," I tell him, "but I believe it. It all adds up. And if you had met that woman!"

"Your grandmother?"

"*Don't* call her that," I snap.

Nate holds his hands up in surrender. "Sorry, I forgot."

"Well, *don't* forget." I sigh. "She called me an *it*, Nate. An *IT*!" I shiver at the memory and Nate slides a comforting arm around my shoulders.

"I'm sorry," he says quietly.

I sink back into the couch and lean my head against him. "I missed you," I say shyly.

Nate takes my hand. "I missed you, too," he says. "I'm really glad you're back."

"Me, too," I close my eyes a moment, wishing I could just stay snuggled beside Nate and rest awhile. But I can't. I sit up again. "We can't stay here much longer, Nate," I say. "We've got to get going."

Nate looks at me oddly. "Going where?"

"There," I say, pointing out his living room window at the mountains, blue-gray in the murky haze. "We've got to get the kids and go."

Nate is staring at me still, not saying anything. I lower my eyes and a lump of fear rises in my throat. "You will help me, won't you?" I ask.

Nate still doesn't answer, and his silence frightens me. I look up again with pleading eyes. "Nate, please . . ." I beg.

He stares at me incredulously. "Are you talking about running away?" he asks.

"No!" I shout.

Nate pulls back, startled by the vehemence of my reaction. I am startled, too. My emotions are running high and I close my eyes and will myself to calm down. Losing control won't help anything. "No," I repeat quietly, "not *running* away, just . . . going away, to start over, and make a new life."

Nate shakes his head slowly and anger starts to build inside of me. "You're talking crazy, Anna," he says.

The anger inside me explodes.

"Fine then," I shout, yanking my hand out of his. "Forget it! I should have known you wouldn't be here for me when I needed you."

Nate frowns. "That's not true," he says. "I'm here for you. But this doesn't make any sense, Anna. What about school? What about all your dreams?"

I jump up off the couch and stalk across the room. "I don't have any more dreams," I say bitterly. "I can't afford them." I fold my arms over my chest and stare out the window. My head feels hot and heavy. But the mountains look cool and gray and welcoming.

Nate appears at my shoulder and stares out the window, too. "Those mountains out there aren't any different from this one we live on, Anna," he says gently. "Your answers aren't out there."

"Where are they then?" I cry, whirling to face him.

"They're here," Nate says, grabbing hold of my head with both of his hands and looking hard into my eyes. "Go back to school. Get your education. Make a life for yourself."

I push his hands away. "And what about Mandy and Casey?" I shout. "Do you expect me to just abandon them, like Mama did?"

"Of course not," Nate says. "But you can get help . . ."

I turn my face away in disgust. I didn't come here to hear the same old speeches. I came to get help. But I can see now that I'm wasting my time.

"Never mind," I say. "I've got to go. Just forget you ever saw me, okay?" I start to push past him.

"No," says Nate, grabbing my arm.

I glare into his eyes. "No, what?" I ask.

"No, I'm not going to lie for you anymore," he tells me. "I'm not going to cover for you the way you covered for your mother all these years."

"What?" I tear my arm away, fighting the urge to slap his face. "Don't you ever, *ever*, compare me to her!" I shout. "This is nothing like that. *Nothing!*"

"I'm sorry, Anna," he goes on. "But I don't see it that way. The circumstances may be different, but you're still running away."

"I'm *not!*"

"Yes, you are."

We glare at each other a moment longer, then I turn away. I stare out the window again, fighting tears. The mountains are growing fainter, fading into the haze. I gaze at Nate's wide front lawn with its beautiful plantings and manicured grass, and bitterness rises inside me again. "You have no right to judge me," I say quietly, "you and your nice, cozy house, and your nice, cozy family. You haven't got a clue."

Nate sighs heavily. "Look, I know you've had it tough," he says. "I guess maybe that's why I've gone along with you this far. But don't go judging me either, okay? You don't know anything about my life."

I turn slowly, looking pointedly at the beautiful furniture around me. I frown at Nate. "Are you trying to tell me you've got it tough?" I ask.

Nate slides his hands into his pockets. "I'm trying to tell you," he says, "that people's lives aren't always what they seem."

I smirk. "Like I don't know that, right? Look who you're talking to."

"Exactly," says Nate. "That's why you should know better."

"All right, fine," I snap, rolling my eyes. "So

what's so tough about your life? Doesn't Mom give you enough allowance?"

Nate looks at me sharply. "For your information," he says. "Frank Leon isn't my real dad. My real dad died when I was nine years old."

I stare back. So this is Nate's secret, the quiet thing inside him. I should show compassion, I know, but it's hard for me to share his pain when mine seems so much worse. "I'm sorry," I say, "that must have been tough, but at least you *had* a father."

Nate isn't listening. He is staring out the window now. "He shot himself," he says, "and I was there."

"What!" My mouth drops open and I feel like someone just punched me in the stomach.

"It happened at the cabin," Nate goes on quietly. "It was an accident. But still, it's something I live with every day."

"God." I sink down into a chair, trying to catch my breath again. "I'm sorry, Nate," I say, "really sorry. God, I had no idea."

Nate sucks in a deep breath and lets it out slowly. "It's not something I talk about a lot. But . . . that's part of what I'm trying to say. Lots of people have problems. Just because you can't see them doesn't mean they aren't there."

I shake my head slowly. My ears are starting to buzz and it's getting harder and harder to think. "I'm sorry, Nate," I say again. "Really sorry. But I don't see what any of this has to do with me."

Nate crouches down in front of me. "I'm trying to tell you that you've got to face your problems and deal with them," he says. "You can't keep running away. Just think. If your mother had faced her problems years ago, you wouldn't be in this mess today."

I put my heavy head down in my hands and try to comprehend what Nate is saying. He is telling me I should give up and go to the authorities. Even if it means losing Mandy and Casey. I try now to picture my life without them, without the warmth of their hugs and smiles, the music of their little voices, the love in their eyes. A great, jagged hole opens up in my heart and the emptiness of it threatens to suck me in.

"I can't," I cry. "I can't." I look at Nate and shake my head. "Other people's problems aren't like mine," I say. "I have no choice."

Nate gets slowly to his feet. "There's always a choice," he says.

"No. Not for me." I stand and the room seems to tilt. I lean against the window to steady myself. The mountains are only shadows now, shadows of the sky. I must hurry. Hurry. Soon it will be too late.

"I've got to go," I say, turning to Nate one last time. "Can you help me get the kids out of the McCallums' at least?"

"No." Nate shakes his head firmly and stares at the floor. "If that's your choice, I can't help you anymore."

Bitter tears sting my eyes. I feel betrayed and abandoned once again. "Fine," I say. "Fine! Who needs your help anyway?" I tear the door open and rush blindly across the driveway toward the woods.

He doesn't understand! Nobody understands! Nobody has my life!

I am raging now, my emotions in a boil over the time lost, the plans gone awry, the trust betrayed. My head spins as I stumble through the woods, hating Nate, hating Mama, hating life. Twigs and branches whip at my arms and face, brambles tear at my legs, and roots grab at my feet. Then something snags the hem of my jeans, pulling me up short and tumbling me into the underbrush. In blind fury I twist around, grab at whatever it is, and yank. Pain tears through my hand and I pause, staring dumbly at the old length of barbed wire fence that is snared around my leg and at the river of red that is running down my hand. All the strength drains out of me and I slump to the ground, broken and bleeding, inside and out.

Go back, Anna. Nate's right, you know.

"No!" I push myself up. "I've got to go."

Go where, Anna? Go where?

"There!" I lift my pounding head and stare,

but even the mountains are gone. "Oh, God," I cry, sinking back to earth, "Oh, God, I don't know."

And then Nate is there, reaching out to me, and I'm reaching back. And then he is holding me and I'm sobbing, "Help me, Nate. Help me, please. I don't want to run anymore."

32

I sit across the desk from Mrs. Romero, slouched back, arms crossed, legs crossed, bouncing my foot.

"Anna," she says. "I told you from the beginning that you had rights, that we were here to help you. Why didn't you tell us the truth?"

I shrug and stare down at my foot.

Mrs. Romero sighs. "Never mind," she says kindly. "I understand how hard it can be. Let's just start over, okay?"

I glance up at her and nod.

"Okay," she says. "Now, we need to talk about the future."

I sit up straight. "I don't want Mandy and Casey anywhere near those O'Dells," I say quickly.

Mrs. Romero nods. "I can certainly understand that," she says. "But I don't expect much trouble. From what you've told me, I doubt the O'Dells will want anyone checking into their affairs."

Mrs. Romero gives me a conspiratorial wink and I feel the tension starting to drain from my body. Maybe she really is on my side, after all. I lean forward. "And I want us to stay together," I tell her. "I don't want the McCallums to have Casey."

Mrs. Romero leans forward, too, and folds her hands on her desk. "Mandy and Casey are already with another family, Anna," she says.

"What?" I pull back again. "Why? When did that happen?"

"Right after you disappeared. Mandy complained. She told me the McCallums were mean."

I stare at Mrs. Romero and then a smile tugs at my lips. "That sounds like Mandy," I say.

Mrs. Romero looks at me pointedly. "Why didn't you tell me you were being mistreated, Anna?"

I shrug. "We weren't really," I say. "I mean nobody was beating us or anything. Besides, we were together. That's all that really mattered."

"No, it isn't, Anna. Children deserve to be happy, and well cared for, and loved. Wouldn't you like that?"

I smirk. "Oh, sure," I say. "I'd like to win the lottery, too, but what are the chances?"

Mrs. Romero smiles. "Well, I can't do much about the lottery," she says, "but I can tell you that the chances of finding you a happy home are quite good, if you're willing to be flexible."

Flexible? The alarm goes off in my head. I sink back in my chair and cross my arms again.

"Take it easy," Mrs. Romero says, "and just listen, okay?"

I frown. *As if I have a choice.*

"Mandy and Casey are with one of our adoptive couples now," says Mrs. Romero.

"Adoptive couples?" I say. "What does that mean?"

"Our adoptive parents are people who are in the system specifically in the hope of finding adoptable children that they can keep and raise as their own," Mrs. Romero explains. "The Martins have been on our waiting list for a long time, and they're just delighted with Mandy and Casey. As you can imagine they are very hopeful that this placement will lead to adoption."

I listen and wait.

"They're a young couple," Mrs. Romero continues, "well educated, with a lovely home. They really have a lot to offer Mandy and Casey. . . ." Mrs. Romero breaks eye contact with me now and hesitates.

"But they don't want me," I interject.

Mrs. Romero takes a deep breath and nods. "It's not a matter of race, Anna," she hurries to add. "These people aren't like that. It's just that they're young, as I said. They want a young family. They don't feel that they're ready for a teenager yet."

I stare at the empty space between Mrs. Romero and me, letting her words slowly sink in, then I shake my head. "No," I say quietly but firmly. "No way."

"But . . ."

"No buts." My anger is rising now and I jump to my feet. "End of conversation! I want my lawyer. Now."

"Anna, wait." Mrs. Romero stands up, too.

"No!" I turn to go. "I told you I'll never give those kids up. I raised them. I've been mother and father to them all their lives. Nobody can love them like I do!"

"Anna, you're wrong."

"I'm not wrong!"

Mrs. Romero comes around her desk and puts a hand on my shoulder, but I push it away.

"Leave me alone," I say angrily. "I thought you were on my side."

"I am on your side, Anna," she says, "if you'll just please hear me out."

I stand breathing hard, arms crossed over my chest.

"I swear, Anna," Mrs. Romero insists, "no one's going to make you do anything you don't want to do. We just want you to understand the choices. Can't we please sit down and talk some more?" She motions toward the chair.

After a long moment I flop back down again. "I'll listen," I tell her, "but I'm not changing my mind."

Mrs. Romero settles back into her chair.

"I understand your feelings, Anna," she says, "and I don't argue for a minute the strength of your love for your brother and sister, but you are underestimating the love of adoptive parents. The love adoptive parents feel for their children is every bit as strong as the love of a natural parent."

I cross my legs and bounce my foot again. "I don't care. They're still mine and I'm not giving them up."

"You don't have to give them up," says Mrs. Romero. "You'll still see them. We require our adoptive parents to permit and encourage sibling visits, and the Martins are very concerned that you continue to be a part of Mandy's and Casey's lives."

I snort. "Yeah, right. Not concerned enough to let me live with them, though, are they?"

Mrs. Romero sighs. "I know. It's difficult, Anna, but try to understand."

"You talked about choices," I say. "What are the other ones?"

Mrs. Romero clasps and unclasps her hands. "Well," she says, "we don't have another foster home that can handle three children at the moment, so if you choose to wait for an adoptive family that is willing to take you all, you'll have to be separated for a while."

"How long?"

Mrs. Romero shrugs. "I wish I knew, Anna. I have to be honest with you; it won't be an easy adoptive placement. It could be a long wait."

My foot stops bouncing. "So basically you're telling me there is no choice," I say.

"Well, there's always a chance," says Mrs. Romero. "Someone could walk in here tomorrow and want you all."

"Yeah, right."

"Anna." Mrs. Romero leans across the desk. "Please understand. We're not the enemy. We're doing the best we can."

I clench my jaws together to keep my lips from quivering. There are no choices, just as I suspected. Why did I let Nate talk me into this? Why didn't I just keep running?

"I'm going to ask you to think about something very carefully," Mrs. Romero continues. "I'm going to ask you to think about what's best for Mandy and Casey."

I stare at Mrs. Romero for a long moment, and then I can no longer bite back the tears. "No!" I shout. "Don't lay that trip on me. I am thinking of them. They love me. They need me. I have to be with them. Don't you understand?!" I put my head in my hands and Mandy's and Casey's little faces swim before my eyes. "I miss them. I love them. Why . . . why is this happening?"

Mrs. Romero lets me cry without interruption. When my tears slow she hands me a small box of Kleenex. Her eyes are sad and I can't be angry with her anymore. She is only doing her job. I'm tired. So tired.

I fix my eyes on the space between Mrs. Romero and me and sink into a fuzzy haze. "What would happen to me?" I hear myself say.

"Well," says Mrs. Romero, "a couple has come forward and asked for you."

It takes a long time for the words to sink through the haze, but when they do Mrs. Romero comes into sharp focus again.

"What did you say?" I ask.

"I said, a couple has asked for you."

I stare, sure I can't be hearing right.

"What do you mean, asked for me?"

"Inquired into adoption," says Mrs. Romero. "They've been following your story in the paper, and they called and said that if you became available for adoption, they would be interested. They came in for screening and we videotaped an interview with them. They gave permission for you to see it if you'd like."

I'm still staring at Mrs. Romero, trying hard

to absorb her words. "They want me?" I repeat.

Mrs. Romero nods, but I'm still not sure I am getting this right.

"Why?" I ask. "Why would they want me?"

Mrs. Romero smiles. "Anna," she says gently, "you're quite a special person."

33

Mrs. Romero slips the tape into the VCR and I sit back on the couch with my heart thumping. Nate sits down beside me. There is some gray fuzz and then the picture comes on the screen.

My eyes widen and my mouth drops open. "Mel?" I blurt out. I look at Nate and he shrugs his own surprise.

I look back at the screen. "And that's his wife, Mary. Why would Mel and Mary want me?"

Mrs. Romero touches a finger to her lips. "Listen," she says.

Mrs. Romero is sitting behind her desk in the video. Mel and Mary sit in front of her, Mel perched on the edge of his chair, bouncing a little gray wool cap on his knee. Mel is doing most of the talking, with Mary nodding her agreement.

"You're not young," Mrs. Romero is saying.

"Who, me?" Mel leans back and whacks himself on the chest. "Why, I'm sixty-one and fit as a fiddle." He winks at his wife. "She must be talking about you, Mary."

Mary Theopolis smirks at her husband. "Old fool! I'm younger than you."

Mrs. Romero grins. "I've no doubt you're both in fine health," she said with a chuckle, "but still, early sixties is not young to be raising a child. What makes you want to take on that kind of responsibility at a time in life when most people are looking to slow down a little, and, well, you know, smell the roses?"

"The truth is, Miz Romero," he says, "slowing down is highly overrated. Mary and I, we raised five kids. Did a good job, too, didn't we, Mother?"

Mary smiles and nods.

"Sent 'em all to college," Mel adds proudly. "Got us a doctor, an accountant, two teachers, a librarian, and . . ." Mel pulls out his wallet, unfolds a string of pictures and lays them out on Mrs. Romero's desk, "seven of the most beautiful little grandbabies in the whole world!"

Mrs. Romero nods her appreciation. "Adorable," she says.

Mel beams and scoops up his pictures again. "Anyhow," he continues, "when we were raising them all, and they were gettin' into trouble and raisin' hell like kids do, we used to think, yeah, it'll be nice when we can slow down a little. That right, Mary?"

Mary nods.

"But you know what?" Mel leans forward and tucks his wallet back into his pocket. "You know what we do now?"

"What, Mr. Theopolis?"

"Vegetate."

Mary whacks him on the knee. "We don't vegetate," she says.

Mel looks at her and shrugs. "Well, what would you call it, then?"

"Reminisce," says Mary. "We reminisce."

"Awright, fine," says Mel. "We reminisce. Which means we sit around and vegetate and wait for the kids to visit and wish they were back home raisin' hell again."

Mary smiles indulgently. "He's right," she says. "Some older folks like being alone, but Mel and me were just meant to be parents, I guess. We miss it like crazy."

Mel leans forward earnestly. "We got a few good years left," he says, "whether we look like it or not, and we figure, what better could we do with 'em than raise another kid, give somebody who hasn't had it so good a chance for a halfway decent life?"

Mrs. Romero nods. "That's very kind," she says, "but why this child?"

Mel sits back again and pulls at his chin. "I feel bad for her, you know?" he says. "What she's been through. She used to come in the store all the time, and to tell the truth, she used to be kind of a pain in the arse, you know—one of them kids who was always complaining? I wasn't always so nice to her. Like I said, I feel bad now. I shoulda guessed what was goin' on. All the signs were there. I was just too big a dope to see."

Mrs. Romero nods thoughtfully. "I can understand your feelings, Mr. Theopolis," she says, "but guilt really isn't a good basis on which to build a relationship."

Mel's bushy brows crash together. "No, no, it ain't guilt," he says quickly. "That's not why we want her. It's . . . you gotta respect her, you know? She's gotta be somethin' else, holdin' that whole family together all those years, and her no more than a kid herself. The world needs people like that. Me and Mary . . ." Mel reaches over and pats his wife's knee, ". . . we don't want to see her get lost, you know?"

The tape ends and I sit silently, looking at the gray fuzz on the screen.

"These people," I say at last, "the ones who want Mandy and Casey . . . I'd like to meet them."

34

I watch anxiously from Mrs. Romero's office window as a late-model blue Chevrolet pulls over to the curb. Mandy and Casey are in the backseat! I want to dash downstairs and out the door and grab them, but instead I wait and watch, scrutinizing the young couple that gets out of the car, judging everything about them, weighing their every move.

They are attractive people, nicely dressed, but not showy. The man helps Mandy out of her seat belt, and then leans in to unbuckle Casey from his car seat. Mandy pops out of the car dressed in a little denim jumper and carrying a doll under her arm. She dances about excitedly, and the woman makes a quick grab for her hand, steering her solicitously away from the curb and the busy street. The man comes out of the car with Casey in his arms and approaches his wife. She smiles up at Casey, then licks her finger and scrubs some sort of speck from his cheek. The man hands Casey over to her and she snuggles into his neck until he giggles. The man then catches Mandy up in his arms and kisses her lightly on the cheek as he carries her toward the door. She laughs and hugs her doll.

I turn away from the window. It was a pretty scene, a happy scene. A scene I've ached for, longed to be a part of. Loving parents. Loved children. A family. Now Mandy and Casey have a chance to be a part of one. How can I stand in their way?

I watch for a while from behind the one-way glass mirror in the playroom while the Martins play with Mandy and Casey, and then the Martins are taken out and it's my turn.

And then I'm on my knees and they are in my arms, and they smell like Ivory soap and baby powder, and my heart is breaking.

"Don't cry, Anna."

I wipe my tears away. "They're just happy tears," I tell Mandy. "I'm so glad to see you guys."

Mandy looks worriedly at my bandaged hand. "What happened?" she asks.

"Oh, it's nothing," I assure her. "Just a little cut. Have you been okay?"

Mandy nods, then pulls away and runs across the room.

I sit down cross-legged on the floor and pull Casey into my lap.

Mandy picks up her new doll and brings it over to me.

"Her name is Millie," she announces proudly.

I take the doll and cuddle it in my free arm. "Oh, I love her," I say. "She's beautiful, Mandy."

Casey reaches across my lap and grabs a fistful of Millie's hair.

"No, no, Casey!" Mandy cries. "I'll get you your doggie." She runs across the room again, pulls a stuffed dog from Casey's diaper bag and brings it back. Casey grabs it and chomps its ear.

I kiss his fuzzy head and he grins up into my eyes. "Casey looks happy," I say to Mandy.

Mandy nods. "The Martins don't make him cry," she says.

"Do you like them?" I ask.

"Oh, yes!" Mandy's eyes shine. "They're so nice, Anna. They laugh, and play games, and tickle, and they read us stories. . . ."

Mandy goes on and on about the Martins and I begin to feel warm inside. I don't think I've ever seen her so happy.

"Would you like them to be your new mommy and daddy?" I ask.

"Oh, yes, Anna. Could they?" Mandy claps her hands. "You'll love them! Wait and see."

"I'm sure I will," I say, "but there's just one thing. . . ."

"What?" asks Mandy.

"I . . . won't be living with you, Monk. I'll be living somewhere else."

Storm clouds rumble in Mandy's eyes. "No!" she cries, "No, Anna. Why?"

"I . . . I can't, that's all. I'll see you, though. I won't be far."

"No!" Mandy throws her arms around my neck and begins to sob.

The door opens and in walks Mrs. Romero and the Martins. Mr. and Mrs. Martin look distraught.

"Shush now," I whisper to Mandy. "The Martins are here."

"No!" Mandy cries. "I don't want them anymore. I want you, Anna. I want you!" Now Casey is clinging to me hard, too, and I fight to keep myself under control.

Mr. and Mrs. Martin look at each other helplessly. It is plain to see that Casey and Mandy's unhappiness is tearing them up inside. They speak quietly with Mrs. Romero for a few moments, and then they walk over to me.

"Come on, now," I whisper, peeling Mandy's arms from my neck. "You're scaring Casey. I want you to be brave."

"I don't wanna."

"Please, Mandy. Just while I talk to the Martins a minute."

Mandy stops sobbing, but she won't let me go. I struggle to my feet with her still clinging to my leg and Casey balanced on my hip.

"Hello, Anna," says Mr. Martin awkwardly. He extends a hand and I shake it. "I'm John Martin," he says, "and this is my wife, Sara."

Sara Martin shakes my hand, too.

"They told us here at the agency how you've cared for Mandy and Casey all this time," she says. "You've done a wonderful job with them."

"Thanks," I say quietly. "I guess . . . I mean it seems like you've taken pretty good care of them this past week, too."

Sara Martin smiles. "It wasn't hard," she says. "We've fallen in love with them."

I nod without returning her smile. "I love them, too."

"Yes." Sara's smile fades. She glances at her husband, and then goes on. "We've been thinking, Anna, about you. Maybe we were wrong. Maybe . . ."

She hesitates a moment and I search her eyes and see the uncertainty there.

"No," I say softly, "you were right." I run my hand down the length of Mandy's hair. "Two mothers in one house . . . It doesn't work, you know?" I kiss Casey's soft cheek and hand him over to Mr. Martin, then I kneel down and take Mandy's hands in mine. I look directly into her eyes.

"Look, Monk," I say. "We're gonna be all right this time. I promise. There are some people who want me. Really want me, the way the Martins want you. And I'm gonna live nearby, and I'll see you all the time, and anytime you need me, you just pick up the phone and I'll be there, okay?"

Mandy chews her bottom lip.

"Come on," I say. "Have I ever let you down?"

Mandy thinks. "Well," she says, "remember the time you said you'd be home and . . ."

I groan. "Are you ever going to let me live that down?" I ask.

Mandy's lips curl into a tiny smile and I kiss the end of her nose. "Here," I say, picking Millie up and pressing her into Mandy's arms. "You go with the Martins now, okay? Everything's going to be fine."

Mandy cradles the doll and looks up at Sara Martin, who smiles gently and puts out her hand. Mandy takes the hand and lets herself be led halfway across the room, but then she breaks free and runs back, throwing her arms around me once more.

"I love you, Anna," she whispers.

"I love you, too, Monk," I say, squeezing her tight, "and that will never ever change."

35

The school bus's brakes squeal and I stand up, shift the weight of my backpack onto one shoulder, and make my way down the aisle, grabbing onto the smooth metal pole by the door to keep from lurching right on out the front window. The bus driver smiles, then leans on his long handle and pushes the door open.

"Have a good summer," he says.

I smile back. "You, too," I call over my shoulder as I bounce down the steps and out the door. The bus pulls away and I let out a joyful whoop as I lope across the parking lot toward the store. I slow as I approach the windows, staring at my reflection in the glass. The girl I see is tall and thin. Her head is crowned by a snug-fitting cap of curls and her eyes, unencumbered by glasses, are large and dark, but it is the way she moves that surprises me—easy and elegant, like an African queen.

Two bushy gray eyebrows appear in the middle of my reflection and I smile and wave through the window.

"Vacation!" I shout as I push in the door and drop my book bag on the counter.

"Hello to you, too," says Mel, presenting the side of his face to be kissed. That is one of Mel's rules. Kisses must be given upon exiting, entering, rising, and retiring. It was terribly awkward for me at first, but I'm getting used to it. Mel is trying desperately to give me back my childhood, and I love him for it, but when you have been as old as I've been, for as long as I've been, you can't go back to childhood again. You can find joy, though. And I think I have found it with Mary and Mel.

"How are the new lenses doing?" Mel asks.

"Great! I love them. I can't thank you enough, Mel."

"Oh phff," says Mel. "I don't want thanks. I just want to be sure you're not overdoing it. You have to let your eyes adjust, you know."

"My eyes are fine, Mel," I say with a smile. "Don't worry so much."

Mel snorts. "Look who's talkin'."

I laugh. "Did the Martins drop the kids off yet?"

"Yup, they're upstairs. Mother's spoiling them as usual."

I start toward the stairs.

"Hey, not so fast," says Mel.

I pause and look back. "What?"

Mel pulls a letter out from under the counter. "This came for you today."

I feel the blood drain from me face. Even at this distance I recognize my lawyer's stationery. I walk slowly back to the counter.

"You open it, Mel," I say. "I'm too afraid."

"I . . . uh, already did." Mel gives me a guilty little grin and turns the envelope over, showing me the loose flap.

I look up at him. "And . . . ?"

The grin spreads across Mel's whole face. "They signed the releases," he said. "They don't want any of you!"

"Oh, Mel!" I jump up and throw my arms around Mel's neck.

The door opens and Nate walks in.

"Hey," he says, "can I get one of those?"

"Oh, Nate! Yes!" I turn and throw my arms around his neck, too.

He hugs me tight. "What are we celebrating?" he asks.

"The O'Dells signed the releases," I tell him. "They don't want us!"

Nate laughs. "I never saw anyone so happy about being unwanted."

"If you knew the O'Dells," I say, "you'd understand."

"Besides," says Mel with a wink, "she knows she's not unwanted."

Nate winks back. "That's for sure." He reaches into the candy jar and helps himself to a Tootsie-Pop. "Casey and Mandy here yet?" he asks.

"Hey," Mel interrupts, "where's my twenty-five cents from the last time you raided that jar?"

"I'll bring it next time," says Nate.

"Yeah, yeah," Mel grumbles. "You kids. You'll drive me to the poorhouse."

"Mandy and Casey are upstairs," I tell Nate. "Come on. I promised them we'd take them to the lake."

Mel frowns. "Now, what do you wanna go there for?" he asks.

"It's the lake, Mel," I say. "I love it there. I'm not going to avoid it the rest of my life."

Nate looks at me pointedly. "Are you sure?" he asks. "It's still pretty soon."

I nod in return. "I'm sure," I say.

Mandy skips on ahead while Nate pushes the stroller and I walk by his side.

"They look great, don't they?" I say to him. "So healthy and happy."

"Yeah." Nate gazes at me appreciatively. "So do you."

My heart glows, lit by the admiration I see in his eyes. We join hands and walk on in a cozy, intimate silence. The sun is warm and all along the roadside violets and daylilies nod in the breeze.

"You were right, you know," I say.

"Oh, good," says Nate, "I love it when I'm right. What was I right about?"

I smile. "About facing up to life. You know what I realized the other day?"

"How lucky you are to have me?"

"No. That I'm living my worst nightmare."

"What?" Nate looks crushed.

I laugh and squeeze his hand. "I don't mean going out with you, dummy. I mean being separated from Mandy and Casey. I lived in terror of that as long as I can remember. And believe it or not, it's not so bad. I mean, as long as I know they're okay, I'm okay. I don't need to be with them every minute anymore."

Nate nods thoughtfully. "Yeah," he said, "makes sense to me. Maybe I can talk my parents into putting my brothers and sisters up for adoption."

I smile and roll my eyes. "Be serious, will you?" I say.

"Why?" says Nate. "You're serious enough for both of us."

"All right, fine," I tease. "I won't talk anymore."

"I'm only kidding," Nate insists. "You were saying your life is a nightmare. . . ."

I laugh. "Not anymore. It was, though. God. When I think of what Mama put us through . . . What I put us through . . . If only I'd known. If

I'd gone for help sooner, maybe . . . maybe Mama would still be alive."

"Hey," says Nate, squeezing my hand, "you did the best you could."

"Yeah." I look at him gratefully. "I guess so."

We walk on in silence for a while. The sky is clear blue overhead, with clouds of pure white. "I thought maybe we'd walk up to the cabin," I say. Then I glance at Nate, remembering. "That is, if you don't mind."

Our eyes meet and Nate shakes his head slowly. "I don't mind," he says. "I got back on that horse a long time ago. My dad and I loved it up there. He never would've wanted me to stay away."

I smile and he gives me a sly grin. "Wouldn't be a silver-handled hairbrush you're after up there, would it?" he asks.

I look at him in surprise. "How did you know?"

Nate shrugs. "Just guessed. It's not up there, though. I've got it at home."

"You do? Why?"

He shrugs again. "Always wanted a silver-handled hairbrush," he says.

I smirk at him. "What for? You don't have enough hair to talk about."

Nate smiles and looks pointedly at my close-cropped head. "Neither do you, anymore."

I roll my eyes in exasperation.

"All right, all right," Nate says. "I just had a hunch you might want it some day and I didn't want anything to happen to it, that's all."

I shake my head again. "You know, Nate Leon," I say, "if you don't stop being so darn thoughtful some poor girl's going to fall head over heels in love with you."

"Aw, shucks, ma'am," says Nate with a grin.

We have reached the park entrance and at the sight of the barrels my mood darkens. I thought I could handle the memories today, but suddenly I'm not so sure.

"Anna?" Nate looks at me with concern. "Are you sure you want to go in?"

Mandy is already running down toward the lake. "C'mon, Anna," she calls. "Hurry up."

I nod to Nate. "I'll be fine."

We follow Mandy down the trail and the memories begin to slip away. The park seems a different place. The mud and the ruts are gone now and everything is green. Lovely white clusters of mountain laurel bloom among the trees. Couples stroll along, hand in hand, and picnickers dot the hillside. The lake reflects the bright blue sky, and from the beach on the far side come the happy sounds of children playing.

Mandy turns. "Can we go wading, Anna?" she asks excitedly.

"Sure we can."

"Yippee!" She skips a little circle around us then runs ahead again.

We come to the bridge and I try not to look down, but my eyes are drawn there, almost against my will. My steps slow.

"Hurry up, slowpokes," Mandy cries impatiently.

I turn to Nate. "Go on ahead with them," I say. "I'll be along in a minute."

Nate hesitates. "Why?"

"I just need some time."

Nate nods slowly. "Okay. You sure you don't want me to stay?"

"No," I tell him. "This is my horse."

He squeezes my hand, then lets go. "C'mon, Mandy," he calls. "Help me push this stroller."

Mandy trots back and grabs onto the handle, and she and Nate push Casey over the bumpy bridge toward the beach. Slowly I walk to the water's edge and look down. The yellow glow is gone, of course. There is no sign that it ever existed. The water is peaceful, sun-dappled and still, adorned by clusters of water lilies that straggle out from the shore. As I watch, a mother duck swims out from under the bridge right below where I'm standing. Three little ducklings trail behind her.

"Hello there, little mother," I call softly.

The duck cocks its head and looks up at me with shiny black eyes. It paddles in a slow circle, hoping for food, but my pockets are empty.

"Sorry," I say, "maybe on the way back."

She paddles in one more slow circle, then gives up and strikes out across the lake. Her little ones fall into line behind her, their bodies making three small V-shaped wakes in the center of her larger one. She could be leading them straight into disaster, I realize, and they would still go, blindly following in her wake, never guessing what lay ahead. Just like Mandy and Casey and me. Maybe . . . maybe Mama knew that.

I sit down, dangling my feet over the edge of the bridge, then I lean out and stare at my strange new reflection in the water.

"Hi, Mama," I whisper. "It's me."

There is no reply. Only the gurgle of the stream down below the dam and the distant strains of laughter and conversation.

"Can you hear me, Mama?"

As if in answer, a little breeze swirls off the water and brushes my cheek. My heart is suddenly very full. I look up toward the sky and blink to clear my eyes before I look down again.

"I went to the place where they buried you, Mama," I say, "but it didn't feel like you were there. It feels like you're here, though. I hope so. There are some things I really need to say."

A young couple approaches the bridge and I stop talking and wait for them to pass. I pick up a leaf and twirl it impatiently between my fingers. At last I'm alone again.

"I want you to know that we're okay, Mama," I say quietly. "We're all with people who love us." I drop my leaf in the water and watch it slowly twirl.

"And I want you to know that I went down there, and I met your mother, and I found out about . . . everything. I'm sorry about your life, Mama. I wish it could have been different. I wish our lives could have been different, too. You could have told me, Mama. I would have understood. Maybe I could've even helped . . ."

Tears slip down my cheeks and drip from my chin, making tiny ringlets in the water. I think about the last time I crossed this bridge, so angry and desperate, so full of hate. I remember spitting on the yellow glow, and the memory pricks, like a thorn, in my heart.

"I know I said I hated you, Mama," I whisper, "and I guess sometimes I did. But I don't anymore." I lower my head and wait for the tears to ebb, then I wipe my eyes and stare out at the little duck family, halfway across the lake now. "I know you never meant to hurt us, Mama," I say softly. "I know you tried your best."

A little breeze comes up off the water again and ruffles gently through my hair, like Mama's silver-handled brush. "I love you, Mama," I whisper. "I love you."

I sit quietly for a while, staring across the lake, letting my tears dry. It feels good to have finally said these things, good to feel, good to cry. Good to say good-bye.

In time I notice another reflection wavering in the water close to my own, a little girl with long blond hair. I am startled for a moment and then I realize that it is Mandy, silently watching. I look up and our eyes meet. She says nothing, but reaches out a hand to me and I let her help me up. She slides her arm around my waist and hugs me tight.

I look down at her and smile. "You're getting big," I say.

She smiles, too. "I know."

We turn and walk slowly, hand in hand, toward the beach. The mountains all around are a deep blue-green. Like great, loving arms, they encircle me.